ICED ENTERTAINMENT

―――◁♦▷―――

EST. 2016

COPYRIGHT © *2020*
ISBN: *9798721246401*

ALL RIGHTS RESERVED. THIS BOOK MAY NOT BE REPRODUCED BY ANY ELECTRONIC MEANS, INCLUDING INFORMATION STORAGE, WITHOUT WRITTEN PERMISSION FROM THE AUTHOR. ALL CHARACTER ARE FICTITIOUS; ANY LIKENESS TO ACTUAL PERSONS IS POSSIBLE, AS THE CHARACTERS ARE HIGHLY REALISTIC.

CHAPTER ONE

"I'm so tired of my guns and my vanity
I'd like to trade them in for some sanity"
Luscious Jackson

I was so close to finishing school, less than six months to go. My high school, Strathaven Academy, a prestigious brick square in a field of dirty snow, and inside - a forest of green blazers. The parking lot was a BMW dealership, lunch hour rowdy with the egos of rich kids, the talk filthy, really foul, the c word spattering across cafeteria tables, the girls more foulmouthed than the guys. These kids didn't care what their parents thought, the parents who would never let them fail.

When failing is the only thing you're not allowed to do, it becomes tempting.

So one day I just stopped going.

I wear my kilt and kneesocks out of the house, then change into my Starbucks uniform in the storeroom before work to keep it a secret.

Every day before I leave the house, I check the mail for green Strathaven envelopes, then burn them in the park with my *Keep on Truckin* lighter with the purple flames. I blocked the principal's number on Dad's phone. He has no idea.

My new homework is to hear myself think. I smoke bowls in my closet then spray a stale bottle of Escape to mask the smell, writing self-questions on pink post-it notes and sticking them to the back of the closet door, then spotlighting them in the dark with my mini flashlight: *What's my style? Who, if anyone, do I respect?* and *What do I want - really?*

Sometimes I roll joints and walk through the tiny identical palaces of Country Hills. *Country* Hills. Right. The only hills around all scabbed up with stucco. Besides smoking, there's little substance in my life. After living a life of people telling you what to think, take that away and there's not much left.

On Saturday night while closing up shop, my co-worker's ex-boyfriend drops by. Trina is a porcupine of a girl with pincushion ears and spiky black hair. She's mentioned Ari before, I vaguely remember, something about a screaming match between them that caught the attention of the police. I watch him talk. He's hot. Tall. Jaded looking. They talk about marriage — they're at that age, they say, where they have to start thinking about it. Feeling like I'm eavesdropping in on an adult conversation, I turn to wipe down the coffee pots, and then they're fighting, fully engaged in what sounds like a fight they've had before.

'...because you're a bitch that's why...' he's telling her.

'Lux!' Trina grabs for me with her sterling silver ringed fingers. 'This is my darling ex-boyfriend, Ari.' She looks him over with a raised pierced brow.

'Hey,' he throws me an up-nod. His eyes are blue-black. They have a vacancy to them. Vacant as in empty, or as in a space to be filled?

At eleven, it's time for cashout. Trina's taking accounting courses so she always does the cash. She takes the lockbox to the backroom, leaving Ari and I alone. In the empty store, Ari drinks his coffee and small talks me as I sweep the floor. He could never work in a place like this, he says — doesn't have the people skills. He says he's addicted to coffee.

'Oh yeah?' I say. 'I don't drink it.'

'How do you wake up in the morning?' he asks.

'Orange juice?'

He half-smiles.

He stays until we close the store, Trina assumes because he's still in love with her two years after their break up. I think maybe he's interested in me.

'Nice truck,' I tell him on the way out as Trina locks the door, his brand new black F150 gleaming in the lot.

The Starbucks uniforms are oversized golf shirts almost the same shade of green as my Strath blazer. The shirt hangs in a bell around the mid-section, making me look obese. Not much to work with. I put an 80s spin on it, pairing it with black leggings, topped off with a high ponytail and thin silver bracelets that slide up and down my arm as I punch things into the till. I like how they jingle. They make me sound lively, alive.

Ari comes into the store occasionally on his breaks; his company is repaving a parking lot a few blocks down. When I see him come in, I crouch down to make sure I look okay in the Baristo machine, its shiny metal doling out flattering, air-brushed reflections. And then, unless my boss is working, I pour him free coffee and we talk across the counter. In his dirty Carharts, he always looks like he's emerged from inside Michelangelo's David - chalked in a light layer of dust.

CHAPTER TWO

> *"Aw just shut up you're only sixteen"*
> **Courtney Love**

'Tall No Whip Mocha.'

'Tall No Whip Mocha.'

And then again in the form of a question once the drink has been made: *'Tall No Whip Mocha?'*

Three times every drink is called. It's the holy Starbucks trinity: Tall, Grande, Venti. Father, Son, Holy Ghost.

'Lux,' Bianca steps on my foot behind the counter. 'Venti skim latte,' she says with clenched teeth. Her face gets red and splotchy when she's mad, which is often. She is trying so hard to keep the customers happy, but I can't bring myself to care.

I turn the espresso grinder two clicks and fasten the metal clip into the machine, the scent of burnt caramel wafting up in ribbons. Love the scent — hate the taste. I look at the girl waiting for her drink across the counter - Louis Vuitton handbag, ankle-mutilating stilettos, resting bitch face, which she is aiming down at me. I grab full milk instead of skim, the steam nozzle blasting the milk into tiny bubbles of cellulite.

'Venti skim latte,' I smile, placing the drink on the counter.

The girl squints in disdain and adds stevia from her purse to the drink.

'I hate this song!' Bianca pushes past me to change the song, *Hot Fun in the Summertime*, which I've had on repeat for the last hour to brighten the mid-winter blues.

'Rayr,' I say.

'You're not even working.' She starts wiping things down at random, the line at the till gone now.

'Time is passing so slowly,' I say, slumping against the counter. I pour myself a shot of frappuccino from the machine with one pump cinnamon and down it. 'God, feels like I'm in class. Guess that's why the pay us, huh? To suffer.'

'You don't even have to work. I do.'

'That's where you're wrong. My allowance is nothing.'

'At least you get an allowance.'

Bianca is infatuated with my school uniform — 'didn't you ever get bored of wearing the same thing everyday?' she asked. For me, it has always been uniforms — berets and tunics when we were supposed to look cute, then later blazers and kilts to mould us into conscientious professionals. Whites for tennis, buns and pink point shoes for ballet. Bianca is from another world. She goes public school.

'Don't you crave adventure?' I ask, opening a fresh bag of beans and topping up the coffee grinder, their noxious scent invigorating the air.

'Adventure? I'm just trying to make a dollar,' she says

Ever since watching the movie *Wild Things* where Nev Campbell screws everyone over and sails away in her big beautiful boat, I've had this insatiable need to be a little bit bad. But I have no dark side. I don't know how.

———

When not sporting my school uniform, I tend to keep it pretty uniform. Every day black knee-high boots, stretchy velvet black flared pants, and black tube tops resembling the upper halves of prom dresses, juxtaposed with four alternating shades of pink lipstick: Bond Girl,

Candy Floss, Piglet, and Creampuff. Quintessential silver hoop earrings. Silver ear cuff on one side. And so I don't look like I live in a winter city, I dye my strawberry blonde hair blonder and try to fake n' bake, but always just burn.

'You're going to ruin your beauty,' my dad says. What does he know?

The fake ID I use to get into the bars says Jayne Miriam Baxter - 23. My ticket into the action. But the truth is I can't cut it in all the chaotic frenzy of the cigarette smoke, breast implants, and predators. I refuse to gyrate on a table for their viewing pleasure. If this is what it takes to be seen, I'd rather be invisible. So all dressed up and nowhere to go, I wonder when my real life will begin.

As Bianca and I are closing up the store on Friday night, Ari and his younger brother, Jonas, stop by. Would we like to go for a drink with them after work? they ask. Ari's truck is running outside, its headlights glaring into the store.

'Come with me,' I beg Bianca in the back room.

'Why should I?' she asks. 'I have no interest in these guys. Besides, you didn't even want to go out with me earlier.'

'Please come,' I beg. 'I have weed.'

An hour later, we're standing under the pink neon lights at Brix - a trashy pool hall straight out of 1991. I fiddle with my diamond hairclip and apply more Bond Girl, the tube sharpened into a slant, which, according to the blog, Pretty n' Pink, means I'm studious and calm.

'My ID,' I pat down my pockets, as we're going in. I check my purse — it isn't there.

'Let's just go in and get this over with,' Bianca says, opening the door.

Five minutes later, we're kicked out, so we head to Roma Pizza next door.

'So you're in high school?' Ari asks.

'Was,' I let him hold the door open for me. '*Was* in high school.'

Sitting across from me, Ari orders hot wings and a coffee. He leans back in his chair, staring me down. He's hot. Very hot, maybe. Perfect ears. Perfect caramel skin. Perfect crooked teeth on the bottom.

'So, what do you girls like to do for fun?' he asks.

'I don't know. Whatever,' Bianca rolls her eyes two full scoops.

A ceiling fan circulates above us, even though it's late January. I'm freezing and on edge. I spill my water, playing with the ice in my drink. As I dab at the table with paper napkins, Ari tells a story about how he went skiing on crystal meth once, then went off a jump, and cracked a rib but kept skiing anyway, bragging without any attempt at subtlety. But it's too late. I'm already drawn to him. He's old, he's new, and he has the most gorgeous shoulders, a little slumped over in this seemingly relaxed position.

'One day, I'm going to build myself a cabin in the woods,' he says. 'No one around. Just me and my gun, living off the land.'

'You wouldn't last a day,' Jonas laughs.

'I'd last longer than you,' Ari scowls.

The chill from the ceiling fan seeps down my shirt giving me goosebumps as Ari drawls on. I picture what it would be like if we were a couple, me sitting beside him in his truck fiddling with the radio, him driving with one hand on my leg. Beside me, Bianca pops her gum, a look of bored annoyance on her face. Jonas flags down our waitress and picks up the bill. The sweet one, I see. The shorter, milder, less hot, sweet one.

'What are you doing tomorrow night?' Ari asks, walking us to my car.

'I have a tennis lesson.'

'Can you actually play?'

'Lux, I'm freezing. Can you unlock the door?'

Getting into my car I can breathe normally again.

'Wow,' I say, checking my make up in the rearview as the seatbelt dings. 'What a piece of work.'

Bianca stares at me, closing her door.

'I mean please, what a loser.'

'You're obsessed with him,' she says.

'I mean, he is hot. Don't you think?'

'Good looking,' she says. 'I wouldn't say hot.'

I laugh. Good, then I'll have him to myself.

———

I have reoccurring dreams of escaping Strath in a mad dash, running down hallways, slipping through vents, and sliding down bannisters in my kilt and tie. Running for my life. If I look back, even once, I won't make it. In the dreams, I have superpowers — incredible speed, momentary in-air suspension, tremendous agility, but also a sense that this time I've really done it and am going to pay. I sit up, lingering in the sensation of the dream. A full on action movie I keep reliving, night after night.

Bianca picks me up in her dad's red Sunfire, which was almost repossessed the week before due to his gambling problem. Bianca, her dad, and her two younger sisters, Lee and Brit, live in a show home in Holly Hills. He left everything the way it was because he couldn't afford to change it — even the carpeted garage the realtors used as their office; this is where he goes to smoke. Bianca's sister, Lee, got the girl's room with the canopy bed and the giant stuffed unicorn, while her other sister, Brit, got stuck with the boy's room, Little Mermaid sheets clashing with the blue and red baseball trim, and Bianca got the basement, the wetbar her personal vanity table.

'Hey girl,' I greet her, putting on lip gloss in the passenger mirror.

'What's good?' she says, getting in. 'Don't look at my skin. It's really bad. I know.'

I look, of course. Her forehead is pretty badly broken out, but it usually is.

'Is it bad?' she asks.

'No way,' I tell her.

We crank up *A Tribe Called Quest* and roll down the windows, singing to our audience of passerby with the emergency flashlights from the glove compartment, trying not to eat our hair in the wind.

Bianca whips the Sunfire through Soco, the its tires splashing through the sun-soaked slush.

'Hey sexy,' yells Bianca to the guy on the motorbike beside us.

But he can't hear under his helmet.

We arrive at work just as Jeffrey is doing this rounds. He tells us some side duties we can do if it gets slow: clean underneath the liquid waste bin, count the milk in the stock fridge. Stuff we never do and aren't about to start.

'Alright girls,' Jeffrey puts on his coat. 'I'll probably be coming in later so...'

He always says this to keep us on our toes, but never returns.

'Okay,' Bianca smiles her angelic smile.

He once described her as a deer in headlights. I didn't correct him.

Jeffrey calls sometimes to say he's coming in to the store 'just to check up on things', then never shows up. Trina is his favorite. She volunteers to take the bottles in for recycling. He says there are security cameras in the front and back of the store, but if they existed, we would have been fired a long time ago.

'So, what do you want to do today?' I turn to Bianca, pouring myself a frappuccino with two pumps chocolate syrup.

Bianca stares out the window. 'Lock the door?'

Shifts are six hours long. Last week we tried to get high off the nitrous canisters for the whipped cream. The week before that we exploded the whipped cream bottles by shaking them, then unscrewing the caps, their contents blasting up at the ceiling, the way Jeffrey warned us never to do. Sometimes, if it's dead, we crank up the stereo and dance.

The bell on the door chimes. It's Buckley, a sheepish guy who works for the railroad. He has an innocence, like he's never learned to hate.

'Well, what do we have here,' he says, hands in his pockets. 'Looks like double trouble.'

Bianca pours him his coffee and wishes him a nice day on his way out.

He grins. 'Well, thank you very much.'

'Nice guy,' Bianca says.

'No such thing,' I say, taking a muffin and hurling it at the front door. It hits with a thud, then drops like a bean bag. 'I mean, it probably would have ended up on the school charity tray.'

Bianca and I burst out laughing.

'I wanna try!' Bianca claps. She picks up a cranberry muffin and chucks it overhand, hitting the Starbucks emblem on the door. The Starbucks queen stares back at us with her indestructible pursed lips.

'You hit the target!' I high five her.

I go to the door to pick up the destroyed muffins, noticing a quiet customer using his laptop around the corner. He watches me pick up the muffins. I smile, politely.

'Hope that's not a secret shopper,' I say, pointing around the corner.

'Dad just borrowed five hundred bucks from me. I can't get fired right now. '

'Chill,' I tell her.

After work, Bianca and I drive around in the Sunfire listening to Wu-Tang and smoking out of our matching metallic pipes — hers purple, mine blue.

We park on a ridge overlooking the winter haze over the city, comparing ex-boyfriends. My ex, Reese, used sixty dollar Nioxin shampoo on his inch of hair, and wore diamond studs in both ears like David Beckham. Reese and I would take his dad's Porsche to the casino at lunch, then ditch our afternoon classes and lounge in front of his big screen, smoking Menthols. It was always a war with the remote for Reese's attention. I once hid it in a silk plant in his dad's den. He wouldn't speak to me the next day at school until I told him where it was. I broke up with Reese via text in the bathroom on my first day at Starbucks. He called me back to tell me he was too busy for a relationship anyway, which hurt, to be reduced from a person to 'a relationship'. I emerged from the bathroom crying. Trina, eight years older, gave me a kleenex and offered me the played out advice: 'there are plenty of fish in the sea.' She went on about how she'd lost herself to a guy once and ended up in the hospital for bulimia. I couldn't imagine it, looking her over. She seemed too smart to lose herself. A week later, I found out Reese had been hooking up with a girl in the grade below us, the whole time. Her name was Mer. She was plain and there was nothing to her. I was offended. I'm still offended.

'He traded down,' I tell Bianca.

'Better than if he traded up.'

Bianca passes me the bowl and I exhale into the harsh cold January air.

'Why do I miss Dexter?' she asks. 'What's wrong with me?'

Bianca's ex, Dexter, had once threatened to push her off a cliff. 'One false move and it could all be over,' he'd actually told her, like a bad movie. Another time he cut the head off one of her teddy bears. I urged her to realize the comic value of these situations.

'It's not funny,' she says.

The buzz from the weed has ignited my imagination. 'I have a great idea,' I announce.

'Oh god…' Bianca says. 'What now?'

'Reese parks his car on the street.'

'Okay,' Bianca says, blank expression.

'How artistic are you?'

———

At WalMart, our skin turns an infrared scarlet under the neon tube lighting as we comb the aisles for supplies.

'Crime begins at WalMart.' I recite a commercial to Bianca. 'Wal-Mart has you covered for all your delinquent needs.'

'This is crazy. What if we get caught?'

'Good point,' I say. 'Keep your hoodie up.'

'Can't you just do something basic like slit his tires?'

In sporting goods, we pick out 6 cans of spray paint and I buy us two pairs of cheap black stretchy gloves for solidarity.

'You really do love uniforms, don't you?' Bianca pops the tag off her gloves.

Reese's McMansion gleams majestic under the all-seeing winter moon, a For Sale sign stuck into the lawn like a candle in a cake, his father always on to something bigger and better, perhaps why Reese is a committed slacker. We stash the canisters up the sleeves of our coats and stay low beside Reese's white BMW, hidden from passing cars.

I slide the can of spraypaint out of my sleeve.

'Well, don't just stand there.'

Bianca looks at the spraypaint can in hand. 'I can't do it.'

'C_L_O_…' I spray over both doors in bright red paint.

'What are you writing,' she asks.

'Hey, what does Dexter drive? Does he need a new coat of paint?'

'Nothing. He's a scrub.'

'Really? He seems like the kind of guy who'd have souped up rims.'

'*Clown?*' Bianca asks.

'Yeah, guys can't stand being called that.' I stand back to look at my work. The 'L' and the 'O' are a little too close together.

'Uh oh. Look.' Bianca sharply inhales.

The silhouette of a man walking a dog appears down the block.

'Guess we better book it,' I say, stepping back. 'It's missing something, though.'

I grab my tennis racket out of my trunk, and take it out of its tennis bag.

'Stand back,' I tell her.

'Are you crazy?'

I take a long swing at Reese's passenger side window with my racket. The glass hangs in a web, then delicately crumbles into thousands of pieces, jutting shards left around the frame.

The car alarm goes off.

'Lux, stop!' Bianca says.

I smash the back window, glass blowing back at me like a sandstorm. I shield my eyes.

Lights go on inside Reese's house.

'Run!' I tell her.

We run down the block to where we've parked the car under a large oak tree. Stepping inside I feel the crush of glass under my boots. I check the rearview, glass sparkling in my hair like freshly fallen snow, and see Reese's mother coming down the steps in her dressing gown.

'Step on it,' I tell Bianca.

Opening my jacket, a ribbon of red seeps through my Starbucks shirt. A beautiful sensation.

CHAPTER THREE

"Don't let it go away
This feeling has got to stay"
No Doubt

It's a harmless crush. Like shivering in anticipation before you step into a hot bath. He gives me something to think about. Something to look out the window and want during these never-ending shifts. Doesn't hurt to want.

'Lux.' I hear my name.

Oh, right. I'm at work. I smile at my co-worker, Phoenix, and define myself quietly as everything she isn't. Phoenix is a nice girl, the daughter of a minister. I found this out while complaining about how Trump preaches like an evangelist. Phoenix isn't a strict Christian, though, and she proved it when she inhaled that nitrous with Bianca and I in the back room. Still, she never responds when I say anything remotely negative, as though she's never thought ill of anyone. We could never be friends.

At six o'clock, the bathrooms are supposed to be cleaned.

'Don't worry,' I tell Phoenix, 'I'll do them.'

I head downstairs with a spray bottle and paper towel and take my time examining the shape of my eyebrows in the mirror. Minimum wage isn't enough to motivate me to clean. There was the one time when I found that heroin paraphernalia in one of the stalls — that was remotely interesting. I watch myself in the mirror as I scrub it with paper towel and wonder if I'm pretty. Other people have said yes — should I go with what they think? Would I be pretty without any makeup? Without the clothes? Without these things I'd feel so incomplete. I feel a wave of shame for the mass destruction of the night before that quickly passes. It's really not fair that criminals are punished for years for decisions that take only an instant.

From my apron, I take out a new lip gloss I bought the other day, Sassparilla, a peachy shade of pink like Lorraine Baines' prom dress at the Enchantment Under the Sea dance. I put it on and smack my lips together. Give the mirror a few looks. I settle on deadpan.

As I walk back upstairs, I'm jolted by the honk of a horn. I catch my breath and squint through the window to see Ari sitting outside in his truck, its shiny black paint camouflaging him into the night. I give him a small wave. He revs his engine a few times, How alpha male. I expect him to come in, but he drives away.

'Ari was looking for you, Lux,' says Phoenix. 'He just came in here with his brother.'

'Really?' I ask, then lower my enthusiasm. 'So what did he say?'

'He didn't say anything, but his brother said he has a little crush on you.'

'Oh really?' A smile cuts across my face. I lean down to put away the cleaning supplies to hide it.

'Isn't Ari Trina's ex?' Phoenix asks.

'Um, yeah.'

'Huh,' she says. 'So do you like him or what?'

'I don't know,' I say. 'He's funny.'

No. He's not.

I sit outside Starbucks counting down the minutes before I need to get out of my car, an old navy blue BMW that used to be Dad's which I've personalized with various love taps and holographic snowboard stickers. Staring through the store's copper windows, I see Phoenix wiping tables. She's covering Trina's shift tonight. Trina's not at work much lately, always studying for some exam, bettering herself for some better life while we all waste away. I look back at my discarded kilt and tie in the backseat. I miss the kilt. I miss the feeling of the felt brushing against my thighs. I used to get strikes for wearing it too short, and then detention after three strikes. Work has lost its thrill fast. The repetitive chores an insult to my intelligence. I slide my hands over the cold wheel and consider just driving off into the night. Instead, I roll down the window and smoke the rest of a roach from the car ashtray. The January wind has shifted into a cold one. I hope for a storm.

Dad's been on my case about applying to universities. All I do is lie around and sulk, he says. I'm going nowhere, he says. He's right. I'm not. I want some answers about life and I'm not going anywhere until I get them.

'Hey,' I greet Phoenix, shedding my winter coat and tying my apron, once around back and a bow in the front.

Phoenix is the real deer caught in headlights. She moved to Denver with her family from Boulder a few months ago when her dad was relocated to a new church. Denver must seem like a big city to her. To me it's a playpen I've outgrown.

'Oh, hi,' she says, sorting the beans into coffee filters behind the counter.

I breathe in the deep, earthy smell of the beans.

'Want to flip for the bathrooms?' I ask her.

'I'll do them,' she says. 'I don't mind.'

She scurries down the stairs.

I make myself a hot chocolate with extra whipped cream and caramel sauce, then change the music to Motown, having heard enough of Billy Holiday's tapioca pudding voice for the night. The door chime rings and Trina enters, wrapped in scarves.

'Just here for my paycheck,' she says too loud, popping out her small white earphones from under her knit cap. 'I've been so busy lately. How have things been here?' she asks.

As if I never leave. As if the store and I are synonymous.

'Peachy,' I study her face. She's not overtly pretty, but covertly.

'I'll get a green tea to go,' Trina runs a hand through her spiky helmet of hair.

I pour the hot water and let the tea steep.

She leans an elbow on the counter. 'I swore I wasn't going to date musicians anymore, but I have a date with a bass player tonight.'

What was it that Ari saw in her? Is she still in love with him? I study her.

'He keeps cancelling,' she says.'Says he's got a lot on his plate. Hopefully he shows.'

'Hopefully.' I put the lid on her tea and hand it to her.

Watching her get back into her old Volkswagen bug, sipping my hot chocolate, I covet nothing about her life. Bass players, accounting classes, scarves, daith rings. Trina bogs herself down with responsibilities in all directions, but somehow she seems free.

I don't notice him come in.

Leaning against the till, he stands expectantly with a rolled up magazine in hand. So. He reads. Large melted snowflakes splotch his dusty ballcap.

'Where's my free coffee?' he asks.

'What makes you think it's free?'

'If you want me to pay, I'll pay,' he says.

'For you 'My cousin and his wife, and the baby. free.' I pour him a large cup of dark blend. 'You just missed Trina.'

'So, what are you up to tonight?' he asks. He speaks deliberately and slowly. No one can hurry this man.

'Well...' I look around, suggesting the answer is evident.

He stirs in his cream and sugar.

'How about you?' I ask.

'I don't know.' He looks at me, patiently. 'Maybe a movie later? By myself?'

He licks his bottom lip, looking me in the eye.

'I'll watch a movie with you,' I offer.

'Oh really? You will?' He fakes surprise.

He writes down his address on a page from the magazine. Maxim. Ah. *This* is what he reads.

His presence stays with me in a mild buzz as I clean out the coffee pots and sweep the floor. I feel like I've won something.

As I sweep, Phoenix tells me about Jesus.

'So do you really believe in the Bible?' I ask her.

'Yes, of course.'

'Does that mean I'm going to hell if I don't?'

We shut the lights off, then set the store alarm and lock the door.

'Only God can read hearts,' she yells across the parking lot.

———

Outside Ari's cousin's house, a small tin-panelled duplex, I look at myself in the rearview mirror, ponytail askew, a light sheen across my forehead, smelling slightly of coffee grounds. I take an Aqua diGio sample from a magazine and rub it on my wrists, powder my forehead, and brush my hair, then ring the bell and look around; there are no trees in the yard. The houses used to be part of an old army base. The January wind sinks its teeth into my neck.

Ari answers the door. 'Shhh… my nephew is sleeping.'

'Sorry,' I whisper.

He sits down on the couch. No tour, I guess. I sit down beside him at a safe distance.

'I'm addicted to movies,' Ari says, 'and coffee.' He goes to the adjacent kitchen to pour himself a cup. 'I don't drink,' he says.

He puts a movie on and sits down beside me, too close, and we watch it in silence. There is a school bus crash in the mountains and at one point, the girl kisses her father in the barn. It's such a quick, strange scene that I find myself wondering if I really just saw that.

I shift my gaze to Ari to see his reaction, and he quickly leans over me, takes my hand, and begins to kiss each one of my fingers. A move, but I let it happen. Then we're kissing. Seems like we skipped a step. I feel his hand pulling up my shirt as he pushes me backwards.

'Whoa, slow down,' I say.

He lets me go, and pulls me onto his lap.

'So,' he asks. 'Are you friends with Trina?'

'I mean we work together. I don't think she likes me.'

'She's jealous,' Ari says. 'She doesn't like it when I'm with other women.'

'So this is your cousin's place?' I look around.

'My cousin and his wife, and the baby. I'm renting a room until I get on my feet.'

The scent of cigarette smoke lingers.

'I'm sober now,' he says. 'Saving money. Working.' He leans back, running a hand through his wavy, dark blonde hair.

He goes for the button on my pants. I grab his wrist.

'I think we need some handcuffs here,' I say.

'Go a little higher,' he says. 'I have jewelry.'

I lift up his shirt to reveal a shimmering ring on his left nipple, its metal cold to the touch.

I tilt my head down and look up at him with big eyes, a look I borrowed from Katie Holmes.

He runs the back of his hand over my push-up bra.

Can't we just get comfortable here for a second?

'I'm not going to sleep with you,' I tell him. 'I'm a virgin.'

'I lost my virginity when I was 14 to my babysitter,' he says.

He tells me about Trina. They were together for two years. 'I loved her,' he says, an annihilation behind his eyes.

Meeting me hasn't rid him of his pain.

CHAPTER FOUR

"Try, try, try to understand.
He's a magic man"
Heart

Joint in hand, I walk the ice-packed sidewalks of Country Hills, the winter sun xeroxing light down onto the rows of copied homes. I gather everything I know about Trina. She was a big deal for Ari. I asked her once what the point of life was, to add my to informal survey. 'Well, you could always off yourself,' she answered. For her, there is no 'point' and that's fine. She says Ari was an epic mistake, but then why does she still pay him attention? I'm beginning to realize — as self-assured as she comes across, Trina is surprisingly passive. 'If Jeffrey asks me to do something in a different way than I normally would, I just do it,' she once said. Trina doesn't bother with petty fixations the way I'm bothering to fixate on her now. But then, she once took off her shoes and socks to show me that she had perfect feet — how certain grooves in certain places made them anatomically correct. Sounds like something he would say.

I sit on a bench in front of an empty playground. The shrunken bright blue and yellow swings and slide look smaller than what I used to play on as a kid. Puffing away on my tightly wrapped joint, I rip open a Strath envelope I've nicked from the mailbox, planning to set it on fire. I skim the jargon...

> ... it has come to our attention that Lux Vada Chalmer's attendance has fallen below standard... *bla bla bla...* attempts to contact legal guardian by both mail and phone ... we are legally obligated to proceed with reporting cases of serial nonattendance... hmm...

For the first time, I strike myself as delusional. This was not well thought out, not at all. So what the hell do I do now to cover my tracks? Call the school? Send another letter? I already sent one telling them I was moving, so why were they still banging down my door? Kids drop out all the time. But not from Strathaven, I guess.

Speed walking down Country Hills Boulevard, my phone rings. He's calling me.

'What are we doing tonight?' Ari asks.

'Oh, hey.'

'What are you on?' Ari asks me.

'What do you mean? Nothing.' I breathe heavily as I break into a jog. I have to get home and fix this.

'Be at my house at six,' he says.

'Okay,' I agree.

Just as I'm about to hop in the shower, Dad calls, even though he's downstairs in the kitchen.

'Want to order pizza for dinner?' he asks.

'I'm not hungry.'

'How about Mexi...?' he cuts out. Only a floor away, but no reception.

'I already ate, Dad. Bye. I gotta go. I'm going out.'

After showering, I sit down at my lap top with a towel on my head and type:

> **Attention: Strathaven Academy**
>
> *This is a second notification to confirm that*

my daughter, Lux Chalmers, will be withdrawing from Strathaven Academy, and will be completing all courses by correspondence. Please forward all remaining invoices. Thank you for following up on this matter.

Sincerely,
Ethan Chalmers

I seal the letter. I'll send it priority on my way to Ari's with a blank return address. They have their money and the best years of my youth, what more do they want from me? I blow dry my hair, and, burnt out now, struggle to draw on my eyeliner. I choose a light blue corduroy jacket of my mom's which I recently drycleaned and dubbed retro. I saw Trina wearing a similar jacket once.

I stand on Ari's porch with my head bowed against the late winter wind and knock. A Chinook arch slices the sky in half — peach on the bottom like unstirred yogurt. A preview of spring.

'Come in!' Ari yells.

I step inside to find Ari and a guy who looks more similar to Ari than his own brother sitting on the couch playing video games.

A lumpy woman on the floor tells me to have a seat. Ari introduces them as Liam and Angie.

'Nice to meet you,' I say.

A baby in the next room starts to cry. Angie jumps up. 'You have company,' she reminds Ari, hooked to the screen.

Ari reaches over and puts his hand on my leg. 'Nice coat,' he raises an eyebrow.

'Thanks.'

He's still eyeing me.

'What?'

'Why don't you put some decent clothes on,' he says.

'It's vintage,' I tell him.

The baby is wailing in the next room.

'So where are we going?' I ask, out of place.

'I had a hard day. Let's go for a drive.'

Ari gives me a tour of his neighborhood with the windows down so he can smoke, a heavy pressure from the mountain winds weighing down the sky. He shows me a small 50s bungalow he grew up in. 'Seven kids in my family,' he says. 'We had to share everything. Rooms, clothes. You probably just got whatever you wanted at the grocery store when you were a kid, didn't you?'

'I guess.'

He turns onto Speer Boulevard and takes me past his old high school.

'I was in the marching band,' he says. 'Trombone.'

I laugh, then stop when I see he's serious about it.

'I could have really done something with it,' he says. 'Started my own band or something.'

I imagine him as the leader of a barbershop quartet in a striped jacket and bite my cheek to stop myself from laughing.

He drives past a brick house on a corner lot. 'That's where I got arrested for breaking and entering when I was 19,' he says.

How can I judge him when I just broke a car?

Ari parks the truck in an empty parking lot at the top of City Park, only one other car at the far end of the lot. We sit for a moment in silence, his presence suffocating me like a sauna.

'I come here to clear my head sometimes,' he says.

He flicks on the stereo. 'Name that tune,' he says.

'Led Zeppelin. Tangerine.'

'Too easy.'

He puts on another song for me to guess.

'Ween,' I answer.

He gives me a lingering glance. 'How did you know that?'

'Baby bitch,' I say. 'Lost classic.'

He turns off the music and in the same swift movement, grabs me. I scream. He's much taller than me, almost a foot in height. Stealthily, he unclicks my bra in the back. I reach around to do it back up, but with my hands behind my back, he lifts up my shirt. He's fast.

'Haven't you ever let a guy see you naked before? Let me look at you,' he says.

I yank my top back down and turn away from him, crossing my legs.

'You're so shy. I kind of like it.'

He goes to kiss me again. I jump and hit the horn.

'What's the matter?' he laughs. 'You don't trust me?'

'No,' I remind myself.

'I'm not just going to leave you, if that's what you think.'

'We don't even know each other.'

'I want to know you.'

I keep my back against the passenger side window.

'Okay,' he says. 'You win. This time.'

He holds my hand as we drive back to the house. We drive by Roma Pizza.

'I have a coupon for a large pizza,' he says. 'I'll take you out next time. On a date.'

As I step out of the truck, he pins me against the passenger door and kisses me so hard I can feel his teeth. It knocks the wind out of me.

Driving home, I feel a new charge. Like the time Reese and I railed that coke off his dashboard - I almost can't handle the rush.

You don't even know this guy, I tell myself.

But the charge is running through my body like a cold river.

Everything in my past becomes unimportant. This is when my real life will begin.

———

February 16th, my eighteenth birthday, and my secret life is still a secret. All the bad stuff I used to do is now allowed, well, some of it is. Since the forged letter I couriered, there have been no more green Strath envelopes appearing unwantedly in the mailbox. A miracle and nothing less. I cautiously feel invincible.

Dad takes me out for a birthday dinner and gives me three hundred dollars, doling out the twenties one bill at a time. 'One forty, one sixty, one eighty...'

'Dad,' I say. 'Just hand it over.'

We share a sundried tomato pizza.

It doesn't take long before he starts in. 'So...' it always starts. Then it's grades, universities, scholarships...

I take a sip of his beer.

'The thing is, Lux, if you don't get into a good school, you'll be stuck working some minimum wage job...' He takes his beer back. 'I'm worried about you. It just doesn't seem like you care.'

He's worried because I don't express terror at failure.

'And I'm worried about you,' I tell him, returning his condescending glare. 'You worry too much.'

———

After my birthday dinner, Bianca and I take an Uber downtown to The Church, a two-tiered red velvet theater turned club. Waiting in line in the frigid night air, I shift my weight from foot to foot to stay warm. Inside the red upholstered double-doors, we check our coats and stand at the bar ordering girlie shots until we're unaware enough of ourselves to have a good time. Standing against the thick silver rail, overlooking the dance floor, I notice, among the drunk sluts, Keisha Millar and Bronwen Chase. Keisha does body rolls in tight jeans. Bronwen is wearing some kind of chainmail shirt and trying to twerk her lack of ass. Men's eyes lock onto them from all directions.

'Strath girls," I tell Bianca. "In the wild. Bronwen pops caffeine pills and never dips below the nineties on a test. She just got a DUI after a stint in rehab in Malibu where she was sent to recover from her ballerina childhood. Keisha has color contacts to match each one of her personalities.'

'They're so pretty,' says Bianca.

Biggie Smalls booms down from the dj booth, the little ball bouncing above his lyrics on the big screen.

'Are her boobs fake?' Bianca whispers. 'What is she, seventeen?'

'All it takes is six grand and a note from Mom.'

Bronwen's Crest White Strip teeth shine green under the disco lights.

There was a time when all I wanted was to be like them. Now their perfection feels kind of binding.

Pretty drunk now, Bianca and I go to the smoking lounge behind the red velvet curtains. On one of the red velvet couches, I spot Trina sitting in a group of friends. She greets me with a kiss me on the cheek. She must not know yet.

'Happy birthday,' she says.

'Thanks,' I tell her. 'I like your outfit.'

A yellow floral top with a brown flared skirt. Even in my drunkenness I hate it.

'Lux Chalmers, you little slut.' I turn to see Bronwen Snapchatting herself by the bar. I definitely don't want to be on her Snap. My exit strategy from Strath has been oddly successful until now, but only because I left no trace. I shouldn't be seen here, but I just doesn't really care.

'Camera shy?' Bronwen asks, putting her phone down. 'Where have you been, Chalmers? I heard you were banging some older guy.' Her skin looks like butterscotch, like she just got back from Cabos. Her blue eyes twinkle with a happiness I'll never know.

'Seriously?' I ask. 'Who told you that?'

'Gossip spreads like wildfire at Strath.'

I may not have been in the in-crowd at Strath, but I was known.

'I'm seeing someone.' I play it cool.

I see Keisha judging Bianca while haughtily sipping her Mai Tai. They are two different species.

'How's Strath life?' I return my focus to Bronwen.

'Shaker last night in the Springs. Major dramz. You know how it is. Reese is a tool. No offense. Says he has gangsters after him. Like — okay, G-unit.'

I stifle laughter. I guess he does.

'So like... where did you *go*?' Bronwen asks, her clear blue eyes boring into my soul. "Like, you just disappeared. That's like, weird."

The music booms down from the speakers, and the room begins to fill with fog. It hangs around us in a thick haze, stinging my eyes.

"Oh, I do school online now," I say. "It's a thing."

"But like... *why*?" asks Bronwen.

I'm not sure why she's acting like we were tight. We've never even smoked a J together.

I gesture to my phone, and turn away pretending to answer it.

Bronwen is mystified. Now that I've slipped away from our circle inexplicably, I don't make sense to her anymore. She doesn't know where to put me.

———

I'm a little disappointed Ari never called on my birthday, but I can't remember if I told him about it. I go into work unsure of whether to continue surfing the high I've been riding. Mid afternoon, he comes into the store.

'It was my birthday on Monday,' I tell him.

'Happy birthday.' He gives me a generous dose of eye contact as my present. 'Wanna celebrate?'

He tells me to meet him after I'm done work at a parkade he's been paving.

'Can I bring Bianca?'

'Fine,' he says.

I've always been infatuated construction sites. When Country Hills was being built, Dad forbade me to go inside the unfinished houses. 'You could impale yourself on an exposed nail,' he'd tell me. 'You could fall through a loose floorboard and break your back.' But I couldn't stay away. I'd dare the boys next door to go with me and we'd throw bricks into the mud and scrawl things with drywall paste on the walls like 'Power to the People'. We didn't know what else to write.

Lately I've been smoking so much weed that being sober feels more foreign than being high. Bianca and I smoke a bowl in my car outside her house. The garage door to her house is broken and sits half open, revealing the bottom half of the faded show room inside, cigarette burns spotting the dingy carpet. I pack more weed into the bowl with the butt of the lighter and take a long drag, inhaling the built-up resin at the base of the bowl, its sticky black lining stinging my throat.

'New shirt?' Bianca asks.

I have on a white baby doll shirt with empress waistline, and navy dress pants, cropped mid calf.

'Newish.' I say.

I pop a red sucker in my mouth and spritz myself with Angel perfume so Ari won't smell the smoke.

From outside the parkade looks finished, but when I step inside it's a total mess. I run in, sucker in mouth. 'Did you build this?'

Ari steps out from behind his truck wearing a white beater and looks me up and down. He leans over to kiss me hello. A long, slow kiss.

'Hi Bianca,' he says.

'Hey,' she mumbles.

He shows me around the site, telling me which areas he's worked on. 'There's still a lot to get done,' he wobbles one of the metal banisters.

I lean against a ledge.

'Don't touch that,' he says. 'It isn't sturdy enough to hold you.'

'Sorry.'

Bianca leaves to meet her friend Sharice, and Ari and I go to his place, stopping at the store for chips and soda.

'You got his?' he asks at the till.

Something shifts inside me.

'I don't have cash on me,' he says. 'I don't bring my wallet to the site.'

I reach forward to extend my card as Ari jokingly glances at the pin.

'You don't really fill out that top,' he says, back in the truck. 'But it's nice.'

I look down at the baby doll shirt, stuck on the paying thing.

He nudges me. 'I'm only joking.'

We pick a movie, something about the end of the world. With Ari's warm hand on my leg, I can't breathe. When he gets up to go to the bathroom, I exhale.

Upon his return I taste fresh mint toothpaste as he kisses me, then kisses my neck, his mouth warm against my skin.

'Relax,' he says.

But he's not relaxing me at all. I'm in over my head. But then something shifts. My desire to be changed overrides my fears.

'I said relax.'

'I can't.'

'Shh... you can,' he says, playing with my hair.

If I stop thinking, his skin is soft and perfect. Just stop thinking. Just stop.

As the movie credits roll, I glue myself to the couch corner. Ari brings me a glass of water. 'How did I get so lucky to be with the most beautiful girl in the world,' he says, lying his head on my lap.

Lighting up a smoke, he doesn't let go of my hand, and we sit in the dark watching infomercials.

———

The Starbucks storeroom is sickly hot and reeks of cinnamon sticks. Of course it was going to hurt. I just didn't realize it would be so cliché.

Bianca enters in her black hooded grim reaper coat.

'So? How was the date?'

I smile.

She looks me over. 'You did not.'

I shrug. 'I don't kiss and tell.'

She looks me over to see if I'm trolling her.

At around eight, Ari comes into the store with Jonas and another guy.

I can't bring myself to look him in the eye. He stares me down over the counter as I pour three large coffees.

Finding a table near the front of the store, the set up a game of crib. I stay behind the counter and pretend to clean.

'Go join them,' says Bianca. 'I'll grind the coffee.'

So I go over and sit down at their table and introduce myself to his friend. Cayce, his name is. His nose shines like silly putty and his eyes are like a girl's.

'The coffee here sucks,' Cayce says. 'It's so bitter.'

'I wouldn't know.'

'Why not?' Cayce asks.

'Why don't you just shut up?' Ari says casually from behind his cards.

I hover in shock, looking at his brother, then at Cayce.

'Fifteen two, fifteen four...' Ari counts his cards.

Jonas moves the pieces, Cayce says nothing. As though nothing was said. Did I miss something? We all heard him say it. But neither of them says a single thing. And neither do I.

Did he misunderstand something I said? Did I offend him?

I look him over for clues, watching him play his stupid game.

Monday morning I sit in the food court at the mall, shopping bags spread across the table. He hasn't called. A badness swishes around inside me, corroding my entire core.

I dial his number and he picks up.

'Oh, hey.' He starts to laugh, his friends in the background. 'Hey, can I call you back?'

'Whatever,' I mumble, hanging up before I hear his response.

He's trying to ditch me.

I walk to my car in a trance, the corners of the shopping bags scratching my legs, the shoppers a nauseating blur of togetherness and belonging. In the car ashtray I look for a roach. Nothing but ashes.

I punch the steering wheel. God, I'm so stupid.

At home, I get into bed and roll a joint using the strawberry rolling papers Bianca gave me for my birthday. It looks like a present — all tightly wrapped in pink paper. I consider smoking it in bed but that would be sad, so I put on a pair of rain boots and a fleece, shivering as I step into the chilly March air.

At the edge of the forest, a thicket of weeds stands between me and the gravel path into the ravine. I decide to make my own path. Taking big steps, the prickles scrape through my pants. My feet slide on the dewy hillside and one of my boots gets stuck in the mud. I try to pull it out, but my boot comes off. I pull off my sock to see if I'm bleeding. Standing on one foot, I start to cry in the middle of the hill.

I hate myself for falling for his propaganda.

I pull out the joint and light it, getting high on one foot in the middle of a hill, exhaling strawberry clouds of smoke. This joint is the last of my weed. I need a new dealer. A new drug... the idea alleviates some of my sadness.

Back in my room, I write Ari a letter on a notepad, sitting at the desk in my room, drinking orange pekoe tea with soy and honey.

Ari,

You piece of shit coward. Your word means nothing. You have no integrity.

Slinging arrows into a void, I crumple up the page and think bigger. He can have the last word.

At two in the morning, I aggressively scrape the frost off my windshield and drive through the empty midnight streets lined with filthy, rocky snow. I park a few houses down and take out my pearl-handled knife. I walk around to the back of the truck and pierce the left tire, dragging the knife down to make a groove. The pressure slowly releases. One slit tire is a random act of vandalism, four means hatred. I go for the rest.

Maybe it would have been better not to lash back. I'm pretty sure of this after I start driving away. I have a knack for bridge burning. I hold the cold knife tight in my hand as I drive home, falling asleep to a double episode of Cops, shirtless tattooed men running for their lives.

———

Three days later, on Wednesday afternoon I haven't heard from him. Before, that would be unbearably painful, now it's a relief. I flip through a **Just Say No** pamphlet I got in Health and Personal Living Skills and highlight the drugs that interest me - Angel Dust, Opium, Ecstasy... I'm not exactly sure which of these are accessible to me. There was a guy at Strath, Donnie De Feo, who used to mix drugs in his basement like an adolescent mad scientist. We had gone to the same elementary school, too, but Donnie was expelled in the third grade for throwing a brick at someone's head. He was in and out of boarding schools and juvy for years, and then joined us again at Strath in the eleventh grade, but was kicked out for selling his Ritalin and other stuff no one had heard of before. I look him up on Facebook and send him the code: 'Sup? Wanna meet up?'

Whatsapp only, he messages back with his number. So I give him a call.

'Hey, Legs,' he says.

'*Lux*,' I correct him.

'Yeah I know, but they used to call you...'

'Yeah I'm aware.' Yuck.

'So you want to come by?'

'Sure. Maybe this weekend.'

Donnie goes over the menu – White Doves, Green CUs, or maybe I'd be interested in some Sputter Bunnies.

'Sputter bunnies?'

'It's a new signature cocktail.'

'Lux!' Dad calls me up for dinner.

'Sure, whatever. I'll Whatsapp you.' I hang up and scramble to put my school uniform back on, remembering that it's a school day. My cell rings.

A baby crying. Kitchen noises. 'Hey,' Ari clears his voice.

I hang up. Not because I don't want to talk to him, because I don't know what to say. The phone rings again. Two times, three, four. I pick up.

'Lux?' His voice is grainy and slow.

'Yes?' I reply.

'What have you been up to?' he lamely asks. He doesn't seem to know what to say either.

'Nothing just chilling,' I say.

Have I been ruled out as a suspect for the tires already? He must really think I'm innocent. I guess he has worse enemies.

'Did you think I was leaving you or something?' he asks.

He was leaving me.

'Well, I didn't hear from you for a week so I gave up on you.'

'I've been busy. I mean, don't you think you're being a little harsh?' He deflects.

'Why don't you come over?' he asks.

―――

My dad's girlfriend, Donna, feeds him linguine on her fork, her eyes in a perpetual state of dumb.

'I love that color on you, Lux,' she says about my blazer. 'It matches your eyes.'

'My eyes are blue.'

'Well… it goes well with them.'

'Lux, would you like to watch a movie with us after supper?' He puts a hand on Donna's leg.

'She probably has a hot date with her boyfriend, right?' Donna asks, taking a sip of wine.

The diamonds on her Dolce and Gabbana glasses hurt my eyes as they sparkle in the winter sun setting over the balcony, her preserved features too smooth and tight. Through the kitchen windows, the clinging winter darkness spits back a double-drawn reflection of us, transparent shapes proving we're only sort of here.

'Lux doesn't have a boyfriend,' Dad tells Donna.

'I have no friends either,' I add.

'Well, you can always make friends.' Dad misses my sarcasm. 'Do you need any money for school stuff?' he asks.

My eyes instinctively shift to his wallet, hanging in the lopsided blazer on the back of his chair.

'Yeah, maybe.'

He hands me a few bills, and I rush downstairs to change. I go over to Ari's in reading glasses and old sweats. He answers the door in his Carharts with no shirt on, his long brown arm stretched across the doorframe. The sight of him ignites and exhausts me.

Inside, Angie is wiping the counter, and Liam is sprawled out on the couch, watching football. I don't want to be here, pretending nothing is wrong. Angie and Liam usher themselves upstairs for bed leaving Ari and I to sit in the living room, the only light on, a dim coffee table lamp. Outside it's starting to snow again, sparse leftover snow. Ari sits beside me and holds my hand. I let him hold it.

'Look, whatever you're pouting about, you need to get over it,' he says.

'So I exist now?'

'What about you? Flirting with Cayce.'

'What? When did that happen?' I pull away.

Is he trying to turn the tables? Or was this really what made him snap that night at Starbucks?

'What makes you think I give a shit about your friend?' I can't bring myself to say Cayce's name.

I'm almost flattered. He can't handle me talking to his friends.

He pins me down on the floor, his mouth pressed onto mine, and tries to undo my top, letting go of my head. It bangs against the floor.

'Ow. Ari!' I push him off.

In my heart, I still feel dismissed.

'Sorry,' he sits up and pulls me back up with him.

I rub my head.

He inspects my face like he's never seen me before and leans back into the couch.

'Why did you drop out of school?' he asks.

'I don't know. I guess I couldn't take it anymore. It was a fake world.'

'I dropped out, too,' he admits. 'It wasn't for me.'

Are we the same? I wonder.

CHAPTER FIVE

"I watched you change"
Deftones

'You little psycho,' Bianca says, when I tell her about the tires.

'I took your advice and did something basic.' I smile.

We're walking towards Della's, five blocks from Starbucks. One of our regulars at Starbucks, Shawndy, (Venti Hazelnut Skim Latte with non-fat brownie) gave us Della's number for weed. Shawndy is a masseuse and works at a massage parlor called Dreamville. She makes five grand a month and swears her job is no different than a dental hygienist.

It's March now, but snow still buries parts of the lawns. The sun is hot today in the cold air, but the breeze is becoming gentle. We walk slowly absorbing the early white spring sun with our pasty winter skin, checking the numbers on each house we pass — their faded stucco fronts stained around the eavestroughs from the spring melt. The front door to Della's is wide open.

We step into the foyer but no one is there.

'C'mon in,' a woman yells from the back.

Through a jungle of plants pushing their way through open windows, we wade through a zoo of stuffed animals and a maze of racecar tracks. A man with a grey scraggly beard and a woman sucking on a cigarette sit at the wooden kitchen table while Della stands at the counter measuring out our eighth. She wears a thick sweater with an oversized daisy on the front, its wool matted like cobwebs.

'Ladies,' she greets us, opening her hands. 'I hope you'll stay and join us for a bowl.' She hands me the ziploc bag of weed and I pay her thirty dollars. She smells like soap and Ritz crackers. From the basement, I hear kids banging on a mini-piano singing Like A Virgin.

A fimo pipe is passed around. Bianca and I each politely take a few tokes, the weed kicking in fast and strong as the bearded man strums his guitar.

Della begins to sing and the man sings along.

Please bleed
 So I know that you are real
 So I know that you can feel
 The damage that you've done
 Who have I become
 To myself I am numb, I am numb, I am numb...

Bianca rocks back and forth slightly out of time with the music like a mental patient. I'm about ready to leave, feeling like we're in the presence of ghosts of Christmas future. I take a hard, unnatural breath, the taste of smoke in the back of my throat.

'Did somebody say *party*?' a woman's voice calls from the front door. Shawndy walks in dressed in a purple rhinestone vest with cut offs and fuzzy leopard print slippers, her buoyant fake boobs bobbing with each step. She usually has a dyed-blue buzz cut, but today it's purple. At first we thought she was a lesbian, but she often comes in teary-eyed over men. 'Always the bad boys,' she says, sadly.

'Little cuties!' Shawndy screams when she sees us, stamping our foreheads with kisses. She then hugs Della in a long, breathing embrace as though they've suffered deeply together.

'This is the most fantastic day of my life!' Shawndy says, sitting down at the table.

'How come?' I ask her.

'Because it's today,' she says. 'Play it, Sam.' She nudges the man with the guitar.

He tries awkwardly for the cords as she takes the bowl and inhales. He has the basic cords down now, but they sound sharp — off. Shawndy sings along off-key.

> *Today is the greatest*
> *Day I've ever known*
> *Can't live for tomorrow*
> *Tomorrow's much too long*
> *I'll burn my eyes out…*

Bizarro World's greatest day ever.

'Lux,' Shawndy turns to me, 'have you ever considered stripping?'

I look down at my A cup chest and shake my head no.

Shawndy breathes out a cloud of smoke. '*That* is what I'm talking about. I feel good now. I mean, I feel *really* good. And I knew that I would! Oww.'

'Well, we've gotta go. Thanks, Shawndy. Della.' I get up from the table.

'Baby girl — you go,' Shawndy says. 'You go live your wildest dreams. Life is a bicycle. Unless you pedal, not much happens.'

I herd Bianca out the door with our weed in my purse, Today Is The Strangest still trying to be a song back inside.

'Ola!' Shawndy calls out.

Does she know this means hello?

A cop car slides up beside us like a shark as we walk down the sidewalk.

'Do you think they're watching the house?'

'Paranoia will destroy ya,' Bianca says.

A scathing tension rides up my neck. I'm not at peace. I'm never at peace.

At home, I check my texts. Jeffrey wants me to cover for Trina this weekend — some charity thing she's doing. Saint Trina, with her recycling and her charity.

The phone rings.

'Lux. How's my favorite girl? I miss you.'

I miss you — so close to I love you.

'What is it that you miss?' I ask.

'Everything. Your smile, your eyes. Come over,' he says.

'Tonight?'

'Fine, don't.' His demeanor changes.

So what — now he's in love with me? Last week I didn't exist.

'How about Saturday?' I offer.

'What's wrong with tonight?'

'It's just tired. I worked all day, and I just had a bath,' I lie.

'Fine,' he says. 'Call me later. If you want.'

'Okay sure,' I lie again.

A meme comes to mind: *Nobody can feel the way you're feeling unless they've burned the way you've burned.*

I've been burned, man. And I can't seem to get my high back, not from any guy or any drug.

———

Ari used to hang out at Rockbar when he was my age, he says, as though his youth is a such a far off thing. He wants to go there on Saturday night. Is this why he wants to be with me? To reclaim his youth?

I spend hours getting ready, hair in rollers, cotton swabs between my painted toes. I pair black sparkly stilettos with black satin pants and a mint green tube top with a velvet Indonesian design — my tribute to Trina's hippie leanings.

As a result of my primping, Bianca and I are late. We walk in nicely dressed to see a trashy punk-metal band playing, the lead singer literally spitting obscenities into the mic. I don't see Ari, but I spot Cayce standing beside a girl with long greasy hair.

'Ari went to call you,' Cayce says.

I wait for Ari with Cayce as Bianca goes off to talk to a guy from her school. Cayce introduces the greasy haired girl as Mila. Her shiny cheekbones protrude like marble-sized cysts and her jeans are too long and have been dragged through the muck of the last traces of snow outside. I shake her hand. Her fingernails have dirt under them.

'Mila,' she says, then turns her back to me and watches the band.

I'm not her type of girl. I never am with wide, sturdy girls. It's a born animalistic hatred. The crowd is half bangers, half skaters, head-banging and moshing their demons away. Beside me, Cayce bobs his head to the music. The silence between us becomes obvious.

Ari walks up, barely looks at me, then goes to sit on barstool a few feet away.

I sit beside him. 'Hey.' I give his leg a squeeze.

'What's wrong?' I ask. 'Are you mad?'

He looks away.

'Are you mad at me?'

'Yeah.'

'Why?' I ask.

'Because you're a stupid bitch,' he calmly says.

'Excuse me?' I blink slowly, on the verge of laughter. 'Why?'

'I don't know,' he says, 'maybe your mom dropped you on your head when you were a baby.'

'Are you mad because I was late?' I ask in sheer confusion.

'I'm mad because you didn't fuck me the last time you came over.'

Mila saunters up. 'I'm going to the bar. Want a drink?' she asks him, her dirty paw on his shoulder.

'Ginger ale,' he tells her, looking me in the eye. 'On second thought, I'll go with you.'

Stupid Bitch, I replay his words.

I get up to find Bianca.

'So he's an asshole,' she bluntly offers. 'He has no right to talk to you that way.'

I agree, but am more perplexed that I don't even know why he's mad. I don't get it. Maybe he's just in a bad mood. Just a moody person. I watch him from across the bar where he stands beside Mila holding a drink.

I wince at the music that sounds like the grinding cranks of a large machine. When I look back, Ari is gone.

'Let's get out of here,' I tell Bianca. 'This place makes me sick.'

As we're leaving, we bump into Ari, Cayce, and Mila - also on their way out.

'Great night,' I tell him. 'Thanks for the invite.'

He laughs. 'I'll call you. If I still have your number.'

He walks away with his friends, their laughter seeming to get louder as they get further away. He pushes Mila. She jumps on his back and tackles him.

Being late. The stilettos. Talking to Cayce... I rack my brain.

I was late because I was getting ready *for him*. I was dressed up because I wanted to look good *for him*. I was only talking to Cayce to be polite *for him*.

I sit on the floor of my room and dump onto a white plate three grams of mushrooms from Donnie. He met me in the Strathaven parking lot looking like he'd just rolled out of bed. The school was dead — all the lights out, all the cars gone. Being back there felt no different than revisiting my old elementary school.

'That's it?' I asked, holding up the ziploc bag of powder, stems, and a few caps.

'Three grams,' he said. 'Want me to measure it?'

'No.'

'Happy zooming,' he said, getting into his white Mustang.

The mushrooms are spindly and boring looking. They smell of putrid rotting anger. Above me, the lights strung around the borders of my room are set on twinkle, eerie lounge music trickling up towards them. I rip the stems into small pieces and nearly gag on the first piece. So much for chewing. I chop them up into dust, get myself a big glass of water and dump them down my throat, shivering from the aftertaste, then plunge my face into the cool pillows on my bed.

From this moment, how can it feel so wrong?

Portishead's wounded tunes leak from the stereo.

I start to worry if I've done enough to get high, my heart beating loudly in anticipation. I put my string lights on discothèque mode and light a large vanilla candle, looking into the Hollywood light-up mirror on my vanity table that shows every single flaw on my face. I used to want to be an actress. I wanted to be in the center of things. To be seen. But those intense moments I longed to live inside of weren't actually intense, they were scripted. Read under scrutiny in front of equipment and bright lights and paid strangers. The moments I wanted, I realized, couldn't be found in any movie. Where were they then?

I breathe in………….and out.

It isn't only me that's breathing — the whole room is alive. The corners of my desk waver. The eyelet pattern on my bedspread swirls. Things become animated, as though a different artist drew each frame, everything crawling into itself.

I suddenly become aware that I'm alone in a quiet house.

Dad is home watching the game in the den but that only makes me feel more alone.

I return to the mirror.

I am pretty, I decide. Like a fairy. I wave my hand in front of my face and it leaves a streaked arc in its path. Tracers. I've heard of these.

My face morphs in the mirror. I'm a different person with each change of expression, each thought.

I think about him touching me, wanting me. I've had crushes before, but not fantasies. Don't have sex, they tell us. You might get pregnant, you might get an STD. But this isn't the real reason. It's the mental act of being that close to someone that's dangerous. Ari and I don't know each other at all and I'm hooked on him. The mushrooms claw at my stomach.

I search the kitchen for something to settle my stomach. I look through the colors of the fridge, and slice some cheddar and a golden apple, then pour some water from the tap. The water splashes up onto the window behind the sink. I watch the droplets race each other down the pane in slow bursts.

Stupid bitch, the words materialize in the glass.

I'd been blocking them out of my mind. After the shock of hearing him say it, I'd put them away. But here they are, slapping me across the face again.

Does he really think that of me? My chest caves. I put down my plate. Why am I still with him then?

Because he's beautiful, I remember.

———

As spring turns to summer, I resist calling Ari. We're not speaking and it's okay. The longer the silence goes on between us, the more clearly I can hear myself think. Bianca and I drive to work with the windows down, the mountain air sunny and cool. In the fragile breeze, I pull up beside a guy in a mid life crisis red sports car.

'Hot,' he mouths, lowering his sunglasses.

We laugh loudly like boys and speed away.

I blare Veruca Salt in the wind.

'Why always 90s tunes?' Bianca asks.

'90s is lit,' I reply.

In truth, it's the one thing I inherited from my mother. I don't look like her, barely remember her, but I was given her music collection.

Lately, Bianca has been finishing her weed more quickly than me. She's been to Della's twice on her own. It helps her do her homework, she says. The letters from Strath have stopped now; school barely crosses my mind.

Midway through our shift at Starbucks, Ari's truck pulls up in front of the store and in he walks with Trina in tow. I haven't seen either of them in weeks. Why is he here? And why would he come here with *her*.

'Can I get the usual?' Ari asks.

'I'll have a green tea,' Trina says, in a good mood. 'We went shorts shopping.'

Bianca rings through their drinks.

'Nice.' I look at her unflattering army green shorts, a tribal tattoo coming up the side of her white thigh.

'Nice to see you, too,' Ari leans over the counter to plant a wet kiss on my mouth.

I pull away.

Blood rushes to Trina's ears, her piercings like quills ready to eject.

'I thought I told you to call me,' Ari says.

'Isn't he shameless?' Trina pipes up, still red, trying to downplay what she now knows.

'So I heard you were quitting,' Bianca says to Trina to diffuse the tension.

'Yeah,' Trina mumbles. 'You know. I got a really good accounting job.'

'Want to come camping this weekend?' Ari asks. 'We're driving up to McConaughy for a concert.'

'I'd go,' Trina cuts in, 'but I have to study.'

'Don't worry,' says Ari. 'She's not coming.'

She looks at him, imploring him to stop whatever he's trying to do.

'So what do you say, Lux?' Ari asks.

I want to slap him, and press myself against him. Both.

'Can I bring Bianca?' I ask, putting my arm around her.

She pinches my leg under the counter.

'Ow.'

'I don't think there's room,' Ari says.

'I don't want to come anyway,' Bianca removes my arm, handing them their drinks.

'I really want you to come,' says Ari. 'But you have to decide fast.'

I scan his face for his M.O.. This would really put a nail in teh coffin of his and Trina's relationship.

'Okay sure, I'll go,' I bluff, looking at Trina.

She looks away.

'Good,' says Ari. 'I'll call you tonight and tell you what to bring.'

'Awkward,' Bianca says when they leave. 'I thought you were over that guy.'

'I wish.'

I've never been to Nebraska. I need to get out of this city where everything is so clean and dead. Dad is working in the den, his papers in obedient piles around him. Beside his desk lamp is a chessboard with world leaders as the pieces. We don't have any pictures of her, in frames or on the wall. We don't have any pictures up of anyone. I sit on his desk and pop my gum. He doesn't look up.

'I'm was going to go camping this weekend,' I tell him, taking out my gum and sticking it in a post it note.

'Oh? Who with?' he asks, his pen still scribbling away.

'With Ari.'

It would have been easier to say Bianca. It would have been easier to say any girl's name.

'Who's Ari?' Dad stamps a document with a dry red stamp – **PAID**.

'My... boyfriend.'

He puts down his pen and leans back in his chair. 'And where did you meet this guy? How old is he?'

He shifts in his chair and its leather scent wafts towards me. 'You know Lux, guys only want one thing.'

'Ew, Dad.' I glare at him, sickened that my dad is a guy.

His forehead clamps into a scowl. 'Don't you have finals coming up? The answer is no. You're not going.'

'It wasn't a question.'

He looks at me like he knows me better than I know myself, that one-eyed stare. 'If you walk out that door, Lux, you'll be grounded.'

I grab my car keys and slam the front door.

CHAPTER SIX

"Heaven help me to be nice to you today
Heaven help me not to be what you became"
Whistler

'Everybody, this is my trophy, Lux,' Ari introduces me to his friends.

I shooting Ari an unimpressed look. *It was just a joke*, I expect him to say, but he doesn't. Summer has just barely cracked, mornings new and exciting with cool, sunny breezes. Ari's friends are Gabby and Joshua - evil twins of Barbie and Ken, Malcolm and Chanel - the slightly overweight couple who will end up in matching sweatshirts, Cayce, unfortunately, and Reuben who, though balding at 25, maintains his youth with dirty jokes.

Ari chucks my stuff into the back of his truck and I worry it will fall out on the highway. He takes the passenger seat leaving Reuben to drive and Cayce to sit next to me in the back. I pretend to read the map so I don't have to talk to him. We take the i-76 out of the city, dingy storefront awnings and litter pressed against fences from angry winds. A giant tanned couple holding hands in bathing suits suggests we go to Cuba, the billboard quickly switching to reveal local news anchors scolding us for not being serious enough with clenched brows.

We gun it out of the city through yellow fields and blue-grey skies, and stop at a Love's Travel Stop for chips and drinks. As we get out of the truck, Ari slides smacks my ass. He's expecting something from me on this trip, and although I'm really not into him right now as a person, I do want him, and the first time sucked. The group is off-balance — two established couples, two bachelors, and Ari and I: status unstated. I can feel their seering judgment. They've done this trip before but with Trina in my place. Gabby, I learned at dinner, is Trina's best friend.

As we get further north, the fields end. I never thought they would. Short evergreens sprout up on either side of the freeway, thin and sparse, with rays of sun gaping between their trunks. Trains, silos, American flags, and churches. Middle America in its boring glory.

Ari puts on Led Zeppelin. I sit behind him, looking at the back of his gorgeous neck, tanned from hunching over in the sun all day pouring concrete. As we drive, the guys discuss motors, hockey, and inflation. I've said almost nothing the entire trip. I'm one of those quiet girls now. I continue to stare out the window. The only thing worse than being quiet is saying stuff just to fill the silence.

As the sky thickens into dusk, we pull up to the campsite. By the looks of all the Winnebagos, I see we're in for a Woodstock.

'They used to call this festival Hippy Daze,' Reuben says.

For some little concert in Nebraska, there are a lot of vehicles. A man with a flashlight guides our truck towards a field where people are starting fires and setting up tents. Ari takes over the driving, telling Reuben only *he* offroads with his truck. He maneuvers the rocky, dirt road with an aggressive speed. We collide with an exposed root sending Cayce careening towards me.

'Ari!' I say, 'watch it.'

Cayce resumes his seat. I hold onto the dome handle for balance.

'Babyyy,' Gabby runs to Ari as he steps out of the truck. She throws herself around him and he swings her around in an embrace, kissing her on the mouth.

I watch, disappearing into the dusk. It's at this point I realize how far I am from home. There's no escape now, for days. The pine trees have darkened from green to black, but although it's past ten, night still hasn't fully come.

Ari takes out our tent, which the two of us will be sharing with Cayce. Oh joy, I'll be sleeping in the middle. I sit at the small fire that Gabby and Chanel are starting. Ari hands me a beer and sits behind me as the others join the fire. I almost don't realize — he's drinking.

'I thought you didn't drink?'

'I'm drinking this weekend,' he says.

Who am I to tell him not to?

At midnight, the air turns sharp. I sit listening to the group's inside jokes, sipping on a beer. Besides me, Chanel says the least, only agreeing with common opinion. Gabby and Ari dominate the conversation, chucking stabbing flirtations back and forth at each other. Bring it on, Gabby flirts, to which Ari responds that he can and will. I doubt they've ever hooked up. Even Gabby's mop of perfect blond curls can't hide her bratty, possessed features. She looks a doll some little girl drew angry eyebrows on. I wonder what Josh thinks of his girlfriend grasping for Ari in wild fistfuls.

'I'm going for a walk,' I tell Ari, the beer bubbling to my head as I stand.

'Where?'

'I'm just going to go look around.'

'Alone?' he asks.

'I'll be right back.'

A light breeze shuffles the long grass. In the blackness of the night, everything is sharpened. It's much colder here than Denver. A bare, empty cold. I'm wearing a winter hat and two sweaters and I'm freezing. I pass other people's fires where they cook hot dogs and bratwursts.

'Come hizzle, girl,' a drunk guy wails from one of the campsites, beside a truck vibrating with gangster rap. Under the tarp is an outdoor living room. A set of camping chairs, a couch, and hot chilli pepper lights strung between a few weak, bent trees.

'Nice couch,' I say.

'Hells to the yeah,' the drunk guy says. He's wearing a long blue robe.

On the couch sit a few smoking blonde girls tucked in beside their boyfriends.

'What's your name, girl?' the drunk guy asks.

'Lux.'

'I'm Kiefer.' He tosses me a beer. 'We're from Sioux Falls.'

I open the beer and sip it standing up, planning my exit as the girlfriends send me snarls.

'So where's your boyfriend?' asks Kiefer.

'Yeah, I should probably get back to him,' I lie.

'Pretty girl like you, he better keep an eye on you.'

'Thanks for the beer.'

I carry on through the rows of campsites, looking into other people's lives. Who are they?

I stop at a large empty canopy lit by a single purple spotlight, overturned chairs and empty beer cups awry, sad trance playing quietly from a speaker in the corner — a ghost party. I right one of the chairs and sit for a moment. Alone, surrounded by thousands of celebrating people.

Walking back through the field, it's pitch black. The night light plays its tricks, shows you shapes where there are none, pretends to change but stays the same.

When I get back, I find everyone sitting right where I left them.

'Nice of you to join us,' Ari says.

I look up to notice that not only Ari's attention, but the whole attention of the group is focused on me. All of a sudden I'm not Quiet Girl anymore.

Later, after a few more beers, Ari slams me onto the sleeping bags and runs his cold hands up my chest. He kisses me hard. I close my eyes and try to forget all the shitty things he's said and done to me. It's easy.

'Do you have a condom?'

'No,' he presses his weight into me.

'What do you mean no?' I push him off. 'I can't believe you didn't bring any.'

'Well, do you have one?' he asks.

'It's your dick.'

'Don't worry,' he says. 'We don't need one. I've done it a thousand times.' His cold lips bump into my ear.

I need to erase the first time we had sex, or at least dull its memory, so I close my eyes and let go.

'Ari.' I shake him out of his sleep. 'I'm not on the pill.'

'So?'

'What if I get pregnant?'

'You're not going to get pregnant.' He adjusts his pillow. 'And if you're that worried about it, I'll take you into town tomorrow morning and get you the morning-after pill.'

'Really? Okay.'

With his eyes closed, lying beside me, he looks defenseless.

In the morning, Cayce is lying way too close to me. Cayce, I've noticed, seems to be just as enamored with Ari as I am. I feel a wave of suffocation from the morning dew inside the tent and unzip the tent flap anxiously as though it's a body bag. Outside in the fresh morning air, I wrap my hair into a bun and brush my teeth with no toothpaste in the woods as the birds chirping in surround sound. Malcolm is sitting by the fire, which he's rekindled. His eyes have a natural squint.

'Morning,' I say, grabbing my backpack.

He holds up a beer in cheers.

I walk towards town, hoping to find some sort of gas station bathroom where I can wash my face.

All the rules I learned in sex ed — the videos, the secret question boxes - I'm no longer sure of what I know. Was last night a mistake? Cutting through closed tents and a few early risers, the path comes to a beach of white rocks. McConaughy Lake looks warm, coated with a maple syrup glaze, but it's no doubt ice cold. The path carries on along the lakeside. Nearing Lemoyne, I see a line beginning to form around what might be the town's only store, a house actually, no different from any of the other houses in town, but with a flashing neon blue 'Cold Beer' sign on its roof. People waiting to buy booze, even though it's not even nine AM.

I dodge the line and walk up a street hoping to find something else — a mall, my urban mind envisions. But there are no commercial businesses here at all. If I wanted a morning-after pill, we'd have to go to

Ogallala. I lower my standards and look for a campground bathroom instead — anywhere to rinse off this filthy tent feeling.

Dilapidated A-frame tin bungalows, left unrepaired, stand among car parts and children's toys sucked into the soil as the early summer grass grows around them. Winter here must be quiet. A true hibernation. An old indigenous woman sitting on her front step holds a little boy in blue pyjamas. I wave. The woman waves back and points me out to the little boy who waves, too, shaking his wrist like a pom-pom on a stick.

'Excuse me, do you know where I could find a bathroom?'

'We have a bathroom,' the woman says.

I hesitate, but since she's offering, I might as well explain myself. 'I was just looking for somewhere to wash up and maybe take a shower.'

'C'mon on in,' she motions. 'I'm Rose. And this is my grandson, Nuk.' She wears a faded, old, pink sweatshirt, jeans, and moccasins. Her and the child have matching pale blue arctic eyes. 'Use our shower,' she says.

'Really?' I take a moment to decide if I should. 'Are you sure?'

She takes me inside. 'Thank you,' I tell her. 'This is so nice of you.' I follow her in, attempting to explain why I'm roaming the streets. 'I came from Denver for the concert with my... boyfriend.'

She leads me into the bathroom with Nuk toddling behind holding up a stuffed bear that he wants me to see. He drops it once he catches a glimpse of his bathtoys in the tub.

'No. Nuk, those toys are for the water,' Rose says. She takes out some of the wet bathtoys, leaving the ones that are suctioned to the sides of the tub. 'Don't mind these,' she says.

'Thank you,' I tell her, shutting the door.

I look in the mirror – I don't look as bad as I feel.

When I step out of the bathroom, revived, Rose is watching The Price is Right and Nuk is sitting at the table messily eating a bowl of Kraft Dinner. He runs this place — his toys hanging from the fireplace and embedded in the couch.

'Do you want something to eat?' Rose asks, getting up and going to the kitchen.

'No, thank you,' I say, starving. I didn't pack any food. Ari told me

I could just eat with the group. That would be fine, if I could stand being around them for more than five minutes at a time.

'Have some tea.' Rose offers me a steaming mug that says *World's Bestest Grandma*.

'Okay, thanks.'

'So, you're here with your boyfriend?'

'Well, we've only been seeing each other for a while.'

'And you came all the way up here with him?'

'Yeah, I know. Crazy.'

'Did he hit you?' she asks.

'No! Of course not.'

'Well, you better leave him before he does,' she says. 'I help girls like you.'

She's convinced I'm getting the shit kicked out of me. Do I look battered?

'I'm fine. Really. Don't worry.'

She gives me a sad look of warning and gets up to wash the dishes. I look at Nuk. He has big, clear eyes and an orange ring around his mouth. 'Hi Nuk... how old are you?'

'He can't talk,' Rose says from the kitchen.

Strange. He looks old enough to say a few words.

He takes a swing at me with his little fist.

'Whoa!' I move out of the way.

'Hey,' Rose yells at him. 'You hit bears, not girls!'

I thank Rose again a couple times as I'm leaving and she urges me to come back if 'things get bad'. She brings Nuk out to the steps to say goodbye and slips me a little pink card with a rose on it.

With two packs of raspberry peach coolers and a large box of sour cream and cheddar chips in my backpack, I slink back to the campsite. Everyone is up except Ari, sitting in the same places they did last night, exuding the same boring yet threatening presence.

'Ari's still sleeping,' Gabby says when I get back. 'Where did you *go*?' She sits crosslegged by the fire eating a grapefruit with a spoon.

'I walked into town. A lady let me use her shower.'

'Um, okay.' She looks at me like I'm a freak, jealous that I'm fresh and clean.

I go into the tent and shuffle some things around to wake up Ari. 'Ari,' I say loudly into his ear. 'Get up. I decided I should get that pill, just in case. Can we go to Ogallala?'

He doesn't move.

It's already 11:30. What's my deadline here? How long does it take for this thing to take root?

I leave the tent, take a seat by the fire, and start to drink, just me and the gang. If I'm going to get through this weekend I'm going to need to be a little drunk, which doesn't excite me. I'm not a drinker, I'm a pothead.

Two coolers later on an empty stomach, I've become somewhat able to separate the group from my hatred for Ari. Gabby and I are talking about how Herbal Essences dries out your hair, and Malcolm is making me a pancake. I even find it in myself to laugh at Reuben mooing at some cows in the pasture beside us. Ari finally wakes up at two.

'Dude... what did *you* get up to last night?' Joshua throws a beer in Ari's direction.

The girls laugh at the state of Ari's hair.

'Herbal Essences,' I mumble, but they don't laugh.

The group decides to walk over to the concert pit. Ari starts packing beers from the back of his truck into a knapsack. 'What about Ogallala?' I catch up with Ari.

'What? Oh, right. Maybe later.' He keeps walking, crushing me like the grass under his feet.

I stop walking and stare at him for a second as he keeps walking. Then turn and, with no destination, walk quickly away, whipping my phone out and shoving in my headphones.

'What's her problem?' I hear Gabby say.

'Where are you going?' Ari yells.

I walk briskly away pretending not to hear but I haven't pushed play yet. I want him to come and get me, but when I turn around he's gone.

The sand on McConaughy Beach is strange and white. I stumble over some large, loose rocks, nearly twisting an ankle, to get to the beach. I want to feel the water. There is a ghost town underneath it, Reuben was saying, which can still be seen when they drain the dam. I stare at my reflection in the innocent, lapping water — the blurred label of my Champion T-shirt shining back at me in bad reception. In a wave of fury, I look around for the heaviest rock I can find and, with both hands, drop it into the water. I cover my eyes as the water splashes me right in the face. Guess I needed a good slap.

I haven't smoked pot all weekend - no wonder I'm irritable. I twist the cap off another cooler and walk along the water towards the stage. The lake is striped white with midday sun. It stretches right up alongside the stage. I hear music in the trees. The bass from the giant speakers rattles my ribs.

'Woooot,' a girl shrieks at the end of the beach. 'I am so high!'

Another girl comes up beside her collapsing into laughter. They approach me clumsily, their hands around each other's shoulders —

flannel shirts tied around their waists. Glittery eye makeup, ripped jeans, baby tees.

'Hey,' I greet them.

'You mean *high*,' they say, holding onto each other for balance and camaraderie. 'We're on mush!'

I look into their eyes and recognize the drug.

'I'm Stacy, and this is Tish,' the red haired girl says. 'We're bffs.' They show me their gold best friends lockets. 'Sioux Falls 605.' She keeps talking like I'm the only person who's ever listened to her in her life. '...because I never get a weekend away from my baby girl but my mom's got her, so we're partying hard this weekend, and we've got lots of beer and lots of food...'

They lead me to their campsite where two young guys in similar flannel shirts roast hot dogs on lawn chairs. I sit down on a log.

'This is my boyfriend, Kyle.' Stacy says. 'Baby did you make that for me?' She takes the hot dog and kisses him on the cheek. 'Mmm... so good.'

I decline and she hands the stick to Tish. 'We share everything,' she says. 'So anyway... me and Kyle have a baby. Tyana, my baby girl. She's one year old. Want to see a picture?' She shows me a picture of a bald baby with an enormous pink headband.

'Cute.' None of them look older than 16. 'How old are you guys?'

'I'm fifteen. Kyle's seventeen. And they're both sixteen,' Stacy says, referring to Teddy and Tish.

They're younger than me and they these perfect boyfriends who they actually get along with and have *fun* with.

'My mom helps me take care of her.'

As the boys gather firewood, the girls and I walk down the beach. A long row of rocks lead into the lake. We maneuver carefully across them.

'When did you know you were pregnant?' I ask her.

'Like right away. I could feel it.'

I don't feel shit.

'Why?' Tish asks. 'Do you think you're pregnant?'

'No. But last night was kind of bad. We didn't use anything.'

'Um... hon?' Stacy grabs my shoulder, the green glitter above her eyes shimmering like fairy dust. 'That's how I got pregnant.'

I have a quick flash of her daughter's picture. I guess I don't want Stacy's life after all.

'Don't worry,' chirps Tish. 'Go get your boyfriend and we'll all chill together.'

'Yeah, okay.' Right. My boyfriend. Perhaps a boy, but not a friend.

At the end of the rocks, we take our shoes off and dip our feet into the ice cold water. The girls can't sit still. Their screeches rebound off the rocks. They try to push each other into the water and eventually decide to go find their boyfriends. I tell them I'll catch up with them later, using my backpack as a pillow on the jagged rocks.

Should I call Dad and let him know I'm okay? I can't deal with all that right now. Lying in the sun, hands behind my head, sleeves of my t-shirt rolled up, I let the sun burn my stomach, which hates me for feeding it half a pancake, then dousing it with sugar and vodka. Behind my closed eyes, I hear beer bottles clinking and boisterous voices over the clinking rocks.

'Cheers, big ears.'

'Same goes big nose.'

I keep my eyes shut, hoping if I ignore the voices, they'll go away.

'Hey, ice queen.' The rocks shift under me.

I lift up my shades to see two guys standing overtop of me drunk enough to make the sound of five. One displays his naked beer belly like a proud pregnant woman, the other wears Tom Ford sunglasses and surf shorts. With their box of beer and fishing poles, there is no chance of them leaving me in peace.

'Hi,' I acknowledge them, and slide my shades back up.

'She doesn't seem too happy to see us,' Beer Belly says.

'Well, she's probably suntanning here and we're ruining her peace and quiet,' says Tom Ford. I wonder what color his eyes are.

'Well, suck it up princess,' Beer Belly says, 'we're here to fish. Bathing beauties or not.'

I reluctantly prop myself up on my elbows. 'What are you fishing for?'

'Whatever's bitin',' Beer Belly says. 'This is Adrien. I'm Hobbes.'

'Lux,' I introduce myself.

'Lux. Like the sound of a whip. Lu-kshh.' He makes the sound effect.

We sit drinking beer and trying to untangle the fishing lines, occasionally wading into the lake to cool off. Hobbes is too drunk to focus on the thin transparent string, so he rambles on about his dirtbike while Adrien and I work out the knots, fishing line around my fingers like Cat's Cradle. Eventually, Hobbes wanders off, a pile of empties left in his place. Adrien's Adam's apple pulsates as he swigs his beer. He has dark, slick Top Gun hair.

'I just got back from a surf trip in Asia,' he says, showing me a tattoo of some waves on his arm, then more waves on the back of his neck. 'I'm into Buddhism, too — check it out.' He reveals a large yin and yang on his back. 'What about you?' he asks. 'What's your story?'

'My story..?'

'Yeah.'

'Well my boyfriend was supposed to drive me into town today to get the pill but he decided he would rather get drunk.'

'Do you want me to take you?' Adrien asks, laughing.

It's getting late, the sun gently sizzling into the lake. 'Aren't you a little drunk?'

'A little,' he admits.

'No. It's okay.' My face stings from the hot sun.

'Do I look sunburned?' I ask.

'You look cute,' he says.

I take off my sunglasses and use them like a mirror, annoyed that my sunburn is making me look like I'm blushing. I eye him over to see if I'm attracted to him. He is hot, but there's no attraction. Ari has dulled my senses to other guys.

'So are you in love with this guy?' Adrien asks.

'I don't know.'

'Is he your first? There's your problem. Girls always get sex mixed up with love.'

The muscles I've been contracting in my chest all day to stop myself from crying threaten to release.

Adrien casts his line out into the reflecting lake. 'Sex is just one of life's simple pleasures,' he says. 'We could do it right here on these rocks.'

I feel queasy. Three coolers, two beers, and a guy who isn't Ari propositioning me on the rocks. 'I better go,' I pass my still-tangled line back to him. 'I meant to get out of the sun hours ago.'

'Hey,' he looks at me through his shades. 'This dumbass boyfriend of yours, if you want to ditch him, we can give you a ride into the city.'

'Thanks.' I smile and feel a rush of mild sunstroke.

'And if you want, we're doing molly tonight down at the concert pit.'

'Thanks,' I say. 'Maybe.'

'Later, Sexy Lux.'

Later, Zen Adrien, I think up, too far away.

I never did see his eyes, I realize. It's like we never met.

———

'He's in the tent,' Gabby says, not bothering this time to ask where I've been. My lack of presence, surprisingly more than my presence, seems to irritate her. She's mad that I have Ari but am not making good use of him. I trudge past the group with a half-wave and collapse beside Ari in the tent. He's sleeping. I quietly open one of the bags of chips I bought. Ari stirs at the smell of the freshly opened bag and reaches his hand over like an elephant trunk. I place some chips in his hand and we sit there for a moment. Our first dinner date.

'Where did you go?' Ari asks, groggily.

'I was hanging out with some people I met.'

'Gabby told me you used some lady's shower.'

Thanks, Gabby.

'She was nice.'

'That's weird,' he says. He slides his hand down my back, and in one swift motion pulls me on top of him.

'What are you doing?' I push him away.

He falls into a pout and rolls over, turning his back to me. 'I don't understand you,' he says.

'Yeah? Well I don't understand you either.'

'Good,' he says. 'Then we're even.'

Does he know what it's like to feel *fucked*? Because this is what it would take for us to be even.

I shove a bunch of clothes and a blanket into my backpack, leaving the campsite without saying goodbye to anyone, again.

People are cooking dinner over their fires as the sun goes down. I walk in a diagonal line through their campsites past the tents to where there's nothing but open field. Without the hot sun to soften it, the air stiffens. I put on every layer I've brought and lie on the ground against my backpack staring at the grey-blue sky. When I'm with Ari I feel like my life is really happening to me. Whether good or bad — it's just nice to feel. When I'm losing him, it's like I disappear. I fall asleep and wake up with my back to the forest. I feel stupid now. I've made a drama queen exit and now I have to return. I could find Adrien. I could leave Ari tonight.

Instead, I sheepishly make my way back to our campsite. Thankfully, Ari is nowhere to be seen. Cayce sits in a lawn chair drinking beer. It's good to see him, surprisingly. He's the only person in the group whose presence I don't feel judged in.

'Lux. Where've you been?'

Hiding from this nightmare of a camping trip.

'You missed Ari. He went to find some acid. He's pretty drunk,' he warns me.

There's an angry yelling in the distance.

'That would be Ari,' says Cayce. 'He's been going at it for about an hour now. He gets like this when he drinks.'

Another mad scream looms over us.

'He seemed okay last night,' I say, getting my winter hat out of the tent.

'He was just warming up,' says Cayce. 'He's drinking hard tonight. You'll see. He's such an alcoholic.'

'Is he really?'

'He had a bit of a drinking problem back when he was dating Trina, but then he did AA. He was clean for almost two years up until now. I don't know what's gotten into him.'

This is the reason why Ari and Trina broke up, I now remember her telling me. She told me once, long before I cared.

'What are you saying? That I drive him to drink?'

'Heh,' Cayce laughs. 'Maybe.'

I feel simultaneously flattered and used, my thoughts muffled by Ari's maniacal screams.

'Ari's got his asshole pants on this weekend.' Gabby saunters up, looking like a Garbage Pail Kid with her fat face full of curls.

Of course Gabby's cool with all this. Cool, unbothered Gabby.

'What's he saying?' I ask.

'I dunno,' says Cayce. 'Sounds like he's that way.' Cayce points over to the stage. 'Should we go get him?'

'Sure,' I say, curious to see the act.

Cayce and I walk through the black grass, sipping our drinks in the sharp night air. We pass a little food stand in the middle of the field, *Tacos and Boysenberry Pie,* etched on its chalkboard.

'My treat,' Cayce gets out his wallet, his little baby blue eyes twinkling as he pulls out a twenty. 'Two of each,' Cayce tells the vendor.

I hold the tortilla tight to keep its hot black bean filling from spilling out the sides. Melted cheese, fresh lettuce, tomatoes, shaved carrot, avocado, salsa. The boysenberry pie warms my other hand, its berry filling inside the doughy crust warm and sweet. The only real food I've eaten in two days.

We've gotten close enough that we can hear what Ari's saying now.

'You *know* it's a party!' he screams, harassing people to have fun.

In between this chant, he spews party calls, like 'yeowww' and 'awoooo' like a wolf bailing at the moon. We follow his screams to a large crowd of people gathered around a fire, Ari in the center. But I'm guessing the fire is drawing the crowd, not him.

'I'm on drugs,' Ari yells. 'Why don't you arrest me you fucking pigs!'

The crowd laughs. There are no cops around. Ari looks over to and Cayce and I and takes a swig from his bottle of whisky, then continues screaming as if we aren't even there. 'Yeowww!'

'What, does he think he's a rockstar?' I ask Cayce.

'I reckon he does.'

Ari walks over to Cayce, completely ignoring me. 'I'm on three hits of acid,' he tells Cayce, his eyes lethargic with booze.

'Right on man,' Cayce shrugs. He's seen it all before.

Ari walks past me, then stops and tries to look at me but is too inebriated to focus his eyes. 'Are you mad?' he asks, coming closer, trying to drive his darting eyes into mine but unable to. *He* looks mad. As in crazy. 'Did you slash my tires?' he asks, out of nowhere.

'Huh?' I reply with big eyes.

'Never mind.' He touches my face. 'You're so sexy,' he softens. 'I'm glad to see you and Cayce are having a good *fucking* time.'

He stumbles away from the campfire spilling his whisky all over himself. 'I'm a thunderstorm, baby,' his parting words of wisdom.

As the night becomes blacker I take a seat alone on the cold grassy hillside over the concert pit, swaying hoodies and dreadlocks below. Four women in red saris play kodos and guitars on the stage. In the middle of the concert pit I spot Zen Adrien getting a massage in an open white tent. Of course he is. I watch the women on stage. When I look back, a girl has replaced Adrien on the massage table. I scan the crowd and spot Adrien talking to a guy in a wifebeater, Ari. For some reason, probably the rockstar one, Ari has taken off his shirt. Why, of all the people at this festival, did *they* have to meet? I watch them converse and wonder what they're talking about. I catch a glimpse of Adrien's eyes for the first time. They're blue, a lighter shade than Ari's - a shade of blue completely useless to me.

'Hey, Lux!' Cayce spots me.

I pretend not to hear him and slip into the crowd.

My raspberry peach coolers have faded in and out of tasting good all day; right now they taste like fermented Jello. I grab onto a stranger's shoulder for balance. I think I'm drunk. Maybe I've been drunk all day.

―――

Although I hear a lot of Ari's battle cries from various locations around the campground all night, I barely speak a word to him. When does he approach me, he asks if I'm mad, then tells me I'm sexy. I tell him I'm not mad in the hope of diluting his rampage. I'm actually not - I'm gobsmacked. Does this outburst have anything to do with me? Or is he mentally unstable? And if so, does he get sympathy points for being not well? I'm mortified. I end off the night lying under someone's truck banging out tunes on its exhaust pipe like a xylophone with Kiefer the teenage pimp.

'Are you and that screaming guy together?' Kiefer asks me under the truck.

'I mean, yeah,' I hesitate. 'Why?'

'Seriously?'

I feel like a celebrity for a moment, strangers trying to figure me out, pitying me with wonder.

He plays Thunder by ACDC with a wrench.

'Tell that guy to shut the hell up!' people from other campsites start to complain.

As the black drains from the sky, Ari continues to orbit our campsite, reminding us of his presence with loud sporadic outbursts, the same verses over and over. We know. It's a party. We know.

At around 5:30, he finally makes it back to our campsite. I hear his voice outside the tent. He's speaking to someone. A girl.

'… and then I broke three of my ribs, but just kept on riding.'

I sit up and press my ear to the tent.

'Wow,' the girl responds, flirting back.

'How about we go to Hawaii and get married on the beach?' he proposes.

He's picking up girls. Right in front of me.

'Okay,' the girl says. 'I think the beach is this way. Let's go.'

I hear them get up and start walking towards the lake. But I already hurt too much to hurt anymore. I roll as far as I can away from Cayce and fall asleep.

Ari lies in the dirt, the drool from his mouth creating a small pool of mud. Part of me wants to lie down beside him and cuddle him back to life, part of me wants to kick dust in his stupid face.

I reach for my leftover coolers — it's too soon to stop drinking - and put on some make up in the truck's rearview mirror, then help the girls clean up. Reuben pours some water in a frisbee for Ari to drink out of like a dog, which Ari immediately knocks over with a flailing arm; it runs in a small stream under his neck. Even as we start the two vehicles, Ari doesn't wake up. Gabby bends down, strokes his hair and yells in his ear: 'get up Ari, you lazy son of a bitch.'

Reuben and Cayce drag him to the backseat of his truck.

In Sterling, we stop for pizza while Ari sleeps in the truck. I don't order anything, even though my stomach is empty and sore. Although Ari has definitely displayed the most insanity here this weekend, I still feel like Ari's tag along child bride. Not that it matters. I probably won't ever see these people again.

On the outskirts of the city, I feel hands wrap around my neck - Ari hugging me from behind. He holds on to me and waves as we pass the other car and we both pretend everything is fine.

Gliding into Denver's green canopy, I'm the first to be dropped off. Ari gets my stuff from the back of his truck.

'I had a feeling you were rich,' he says, seeing my house, 'but not this rich.'

We both look up at my cookie-cutter suburban home. I had never looked at it that way.

'I'll call you,' he says, his eyebrows slightly turned up in the middle like a child pushing for sympathy.

'K.' I look into the two-way mirror of his eyes.

And with no kiss goodbye, I watch him drive away. Released from the pressure of his friends liking me, from his expectations. From everything I thought I wanted.

CHAPTER SEVEN

"When the rain washes you clean you'll know"
Fleetwood Mac

'And he kept saying: *you know it's a party*,' I tell Bianca in choppy details, pacing across her basement living room with a lit joint.

'That's hilarious,' she laughs from the couch. 'I mean, you do realize it's funny, right? That he was running around screaming?'

'Well, it wasn't funny at the time.' Those screams, even now, feel like sharp pretzels swallowed whole.

It's been a week and he hasn't called. Dad hasn't spoken to me since I've been back either. I've given him the silent treatment a million times, but never once has he given it to me. It's unsettling.

I want to text Ari but have nothing to say. Maybe we really have nothing anymore. Things couldn't have been worse last weekend. But my feelings for him are complex and I don't really understand them.

'Lux,' Bianca says. 'Don't do this to yourself.'

'How can you say that?' I grind the finished joint into an ashtray on the wetbar, and swivel around to face her from a black leather stool. 'I can't pretend I don't care.'

'What does he have that's worth caring about?'

'It's not that easy. I can't just make myself forget.'

'You don't even try to be happy.'

'I'm not.'

'Bitch, you gots ta chill,' she says. 'Here...' She passes me her little purple pipe.

'Thanks.' I light the weed and hold my lighter over the bowl, kicking off my flip flops and sliding onto the couch beside her. 'You would think I'd be repelled by him by now.'

'You would think,' she agrees.

I dial Ari from Bianca's home phone.

'Hello?' he picks up.

Now he's forced to talk to me. I take the phone into Bianca's room.

'I gave Cayce your number,' he says.

'What the fuck, Ari? Why?' I can't believe he's starting in on this again. '*Why* would you do that, Ari?'

'Looked like you two were getting along. I wasn't going to deny him of that.'

'Look - obviously you don't get it, Ari - there is *nothing* going on between Cayce and I.'

'Yeah, well what am I supposed to do?' he asks. 'Just roll with the punches?'

'What punches?'

He hangs up.

He's leaving me. He's made that clear. I had my chance to leave him but chose instead to get dumped.

'Dunzo?' Bianca asks.

I nod. 'I can't feel this way right now,' I manage, between tears. 'I need something. Anything.'

'I have to open with Jeffrey tomorrow morning.'

'Look at me,' I shriek. 'I'm a mess. Just come with me and we'll pick something up. Please.'

'Aren't you supposed to be grounded?'

'Whatever.'

'Who are we going to get it from?' she asks.

'I know this guy...'

Donnie will meet us on the edge of the city where Bianca and I will follow him to his parent's house in the country. On the side of the freeway, he leans against his Mustang having a smoke. Even in the dark I notice his unkemptness: bruise-colored circles under his eyes, bedhead, scruffy overgrown mutton chops.

'Follow me,' Donnie says.

We follow him through unlit country roads, dipping up and down rollercoaster hills. Donnie drives like a teenage drug dealer. Although he's trying to impress us, he loses us. I pull over on the shoulder and try to read the little green range road signs:

'Springhaven, Springdale… Yeah, I have no idea where we are.'

'I knew this was a bad idea,' Bianca says.

'He'll come back,' I assure her.

It's midnight and we're stranded in the middle of the freeway. But I have to get high tonight.

Donnie comes back ten minutes later, blaming us for not keeping up. 'Man,' he says, 'girls are the worst drivers.'

'Yeah, well this isn't the Indy,' I say.

Finally, we pull up to an outstretched bungalow with a wraparound driveway and four car garage. Donnie's parents are out of town for the weekend. We take off our shoes and enter through the kitchen, a group of eight or nine guys lounging around, some drinking, some smoking, some about to pass out. I recognize most of them from school. Donnie's drones.

'Legs,' Jordie Shaw looks up from his nap. 'Where have you been, girl?'

'Hey, Jordie.' I pat him on the head as I fish for my wallet inside my purse. These guys weren't of interest to me in high school and they aren't now.

'Did you drop out or what?' Jordie persists. 'You left us.'

'I'm on sabbatical,' I tell him.

'So girls…' Donnie opens his hands godfather style. 'What'll it be?'

'Molly,' I tell him.

'No problem,' he says. 'That'll be 20 bucks a pop.' He produces a two small pills from an upper cabinet over the sink.

'We'll take two each,' I say, fairly sure he's ripping us off. I don't have time to shop around for a deal. I place my money on the marble counter.

'Lux!' Jeremy Keegan drunkenly shouts from across the room. 'I thought you were dead!'

'Little lady,' another kid, Kyle Stevens, tries to point at me, but he's too wasted. '*You* are in big trouble.'

'Guys, leave her alone,' says Donnie.

Donnie didn't leave Strath of his own regard, but he set the stage to get kicked out. Now he does auxiliary learning, whatever that is.

He takes the bills. 'So why'd you do it?' he asks. 'They don't like kids like us, huh? Who don't jump at rewards.'

Kids like *us*.

'I was just ...busy.'

'Too busy for school?' Kyle Stevens chimes in.

Pill in palm, I look at Bianca. 'Final boarding call.'

'I don't want to go into work all sketchy tomorrow morning,' she says.

'Fine.' I swallow my pill dry. 'I'll do it by myself. Where can I get a water around here?'

Kyle hands me a Dasani.

'Ew, not that water.'

'Now you're a water snob, too?' Kyle judges me.

'She's too good for us,' says Jeremy.

'Jeremy, shut up.' I stroke his hair out of his eyes.

'You shut up.' He shakes himself loose.

Donnie sits at the round glass table cutting up powder as the guys do Jagger bombs, a deck of cards scattered; they've been playing, but are too drunk to remember what. Bianca has taken a seat beside Donnie where she's interrogating him about how he mixes his drugs. Donnie rattles off information like it's his major, talking about molecular structures and methylenediox something — a private school dork for life. The kitchen's track lighting sears into me from above, dissolving the ecstasy into my bloodstream. I follow some echoing voices down the hall. Am I high already? No - it's an indoor pool.

The pool is domed with glass panels like a greenhouse. I look up into the starred country sky and take a deep breath of chlorine air. Last weekend at this time I was the invisible girlfriend of the wild beast. Now, I'm free from that hell. But somehow I feel worse. That weekend, I was gambling — now I've lost.

Two guys sit on posh red pool furniture, another floats on an inner tube in the pool. Feeling a little dizzy, I take a seat on the padded cover of the closed hot tub and drink my water.

'Hey,' the guy in the pool says, his voice echoing sweetly from far away. He's wearing sunglasses and holding a martini. Looking like modern art, he matches the house.

I remember I have sunglasses in my purse and put them on. 'Nice day,' I reply, sprawling out across the hot tub lid, staring up at the stars. 'How's the water?'

'Not bad,' he says. 'Why don't you hop in? Borrow one of Kelly's suits.'

Kelly is Donnie's little sister. In elementary, I used to read to her at lunch to help her with her speech impediment. Now she's nicknamed 'Dee' for her D cup breasts.

'I wouldn't have the tits for it,' I say, my voice turning to liquid as it bounces off the glass walls.

The guy in the pool paddles himself around with one hand sipping from his martini with the other.

I kind of want to get into the pool but the other guys on the pool furniture are sketching me out with their hoods pulled down over their eyes like mannequin gangsters. 'What's wrong with them?' I whisper loudly to the guy in the pool.

'Mike's tripping out,' he says. 'And Vlad doesn't do drugs.'

'Oh,' I say, more slowly than usual, savoring the echoes of my words against the glass. 'They're not in the zzzone.'

My stomach twists inside me. I hop down off the hot tub lid.

'Where are you going?' the guy in the pool asks.

'I don't know,' I tell him.

I walk down a dimly lit hall to find a bathroom. I remember seeing one by the front door when we came in but then I'd have to walk past those goons in the kitchen. I try a door on my right and flick the lights on to what must be Donnie's parents' bathroom — the largest bathroom I've ever seen. Elliptical in front of an HD screen, massive stone shower, clawfoot tub, marble fireplace, double sinks, plush golden towels, onyx lit walls. The room must have been designed by Donnie's mom. No man in his right mind would want to spend this much time in a bathroom. But there's no toilet. I eye four closed doors. I open the first — a walk in closet, then the second – another closet, but bigger. The third door is a win. I swiftly puke my guts out.

I wash up in one of the sinks with a bar of eucalyptus soap and curl up on a furry white rug, running my hands through it and marvelling at the bathroom palace. Donnie's mom must hide out here. I would.

'Bianca!' I yell, then text her.

She finds the bathroom.

'Whoa,' she says, looking around.

'I know.'

'Are you high?' she asks.

'I just feel... good.'

She sits beside me on the white rug.

'I want to live here,' she says.

'Right?'

I take the rug and hop into the sunken stone tub. Bianca steps in carefully beside me as if it's actually full of hot water.

'Are you okay?' she asks.

'I'm better than okay,' I shiver. 'I'm high on ecstasy.'

'But like are you *okay* okay?'

'I'm over him. Okay, that's a lie. I feel wretched.'

The sun starts to shine through the glass block windows above the tub.

Bianca braids the threads on the rug. 'How did your mom die?' she asks.

'She killed herself. I told you.'

'But how?'

'I was five. She was depressed. She was always in her room. The curtains would be closed. I would go and lie in there with her and look at my books with a flashlight under the covers. One day the door was locked. She hung herself. It's not common, I guess.'

'What about your dad?'

'I don't know. He was always a drinker. He drank more. He's just... what you get is what you get with him.'

'What do you mean?'

'I mean it didn't change him.'

'Did he cheat?'

'I don't know. I was five.'

It's beyond my ability to imagine my parents' relationship; I have a mental block. The few scenarios I remember with her just keep repeating. The tea party under that baby blanket tent, that one repeats the most. It's like being stuck in an endless loop I can't get out of.

'Check this out,' I say, as light from the sunrise slips through the horizontal blinds. I get up and go to open the fourth door. It's the door to Donnie's parent's room. I turn on the light. Clothes everywhere, unmade bed, expensive things in disarray.

'First world problems,' Bianca laughs.

We wade through the clutter into another hallway. On the next door is a plaque with the name *Kelly* cradled between two ballet slippers. We open the door. Candy-colored clothing strewn over pearl bedposts and a pink divan. Pictures of the beautiful Kelly in her ballet costumes framed above the mirror. Pretty, sweet, and rich — everything I'm supposed to be.

'Check it out,' I open the closet. Rows of designer bags.

'Must be nice,' Bianca says. Her dad usually pays the monthly bills with seconds to spare. I have a safety net she doesn't, I'm well aware, but I'm also aware that Dad's money is not my own.

I try on an Alma BB handbag in Damier Ebène. 'Do I look unapproachable?' I strike a pose.

Back in the kitchen, Donnie is passed out at the glass table, his head hanging awkwardly back over his chair, his legs up on the table, a clear tube hanging out of his mouth from a bong shaped like Buddha. Vlad storms in.

'Donnie! Your drunk-ass friend, Reese, just smoked up in my car. That is fucking uncool.'

I have a flashback of Reese's perfectly coiffed blonde spikes and his mangled car.

'Whoa, chill, Vlad.' Donnie tries to open his eyelids and fails.

'My parents are gonna be pissed.'

'Come on, let's bounce,' I tell Bianca. 'Reese is here.'

'*The* Reese?'

'Catch you on the flipside,' I tell Donnie, grabbing her hand.

The guys protest Bianca and I leaving in the midst of their long weekend bender, trying to lock the door as we leave, but we slip past them. My name will be dropped around school the following week — a rare sighting.

Let them talk.

In my bed, I drift into a shallow sleep with Fleetwood Mac playing low in the background, a thin enough sleep to know that I'm not really sleeping. Colors dance kaleidoscopically to the music behind my eyes. I have a vision of Ari and I under a white sky walking through an abandoned grey electrical plant and swinging on an empty playground. He feels not quite, but almost familiar to me. It reminds me of a line in the book I just read. I grasp for the quote but can't remember it. Something like:

Never does she feel so in love as when the familiarity of her past infuses with the novelty of her new love.

Am I living out an old, unfinished pattern? Is it all a curse? What was going through her mind that day? Was it the same with them?

I get out of bed and dig a picture of her out of my lingerie drawer, her calm eyes chalked in blue. When she died, she left the entire world. When someone leaves you, they choose to die to you alone.

CHAPTER EIGHT

> *"Here I go again I see my crystal visions"*
> **Fleetwood Mac**

The future is set. I will work at Dad's law firm for the rest of summer, then get my GED in the fall. When Dad found the pills in my purse, he called the school to check on my attendance, and my fantasy world collapsed in a day.

He sat me down and read me my rights, but for some reason, maybe defeat, he took it easy on me. Then again, the firm is basically prison, and doing school online seems pretty much impossible from the poorly written, convoluted lesson plans and archaic software. He gave me a generic lecture about how I had to 'get my life together' so I wouldn't be a 'lost cause'.

'How will I ever explain this to people? '
'Who? It's none of their business.'
'What were you thinking?'
'I saved my wages from working.'
'It's below you,' he said. 'It's below *us*.'

In the weak morning sun, I watch worn-out businesswoman canter past me across the crosswalk as the WALK sign shuts off. My job at the firm leaves me unoccupied most of the time. I feel like I should be working, but when I ask for things to do, Dad just tells me to open the mail (which I've always already done). This business of looking busy — this is what he considers a good job. My suburban subconscious tries to assure me that the dullness is a sign of security. I take my time crossing the street as the red hand blinks in my face. *Don't. Don't. Don't.* I walk slowly, one foot in front of the other, the cars staring me down, the buildings stealing my Vitamin D. In the lobby of the building I switch my Pumas for heels and wish I had a pendant full of coke under my blouse like Sarah Michelle Gellar in Cruel Intentions. I check out my profile in the corners of the bronze mirrored elevator walls and decide which is my masculine side. The left side.

Shoving my purse under my desk, I go to the bathroom and stare at my tired, bloodshot eyes in the mirror. This is the other twist to the torture — not falling asleep. I have to be up by at least 6:30 to leave time for the commute, Dad is already at the office by 6:00, some human hybrid I must not be related to. Sleepwalking to the staff kitchen, I mix myself an extra strong cup of Tang in a coffee mug. The most essential part of being an office person is not what you do, but looking like you're doing things.

'Dad,' I knock on his door. 'Anything for me to do?' I collapse into one of his green leather chairs.

Dad has lucrative ways of explaining things. He's a master calibrator. I've never had that finesse. Life, for me, has always felt heavy — much too heavy to juggle.

'Open the mail.'

'Dunzo.'

'Stamped and stapled?'

'And I still have all my fingers.' I show him.

'Great,' he says. 'I'll let you know if something comes up.'

As though I've just auditioned for a role and didn't get the part. I pick up the fool's gold paper weight on his desk and walk to his window, the forbidden warm weather only a pane away. I make a handprint on the window, a perfect high five against the infinite sky. *I was here.*

'Lux,' he says, annoyed, flipping through his papers. 'I need you to be a self-starter.'

I leave him alone and head back to my desk where I pretend to write letters by putting 'Dear' and a random name at the top of the page, then record random thoughts in purposely illegible handwriting. All I have are my thoughts here; not to think is too much like being dead.

I jot down the V.C. Andrews novel of my life. A mother dead from a mysterious tragedy, a distant father who can't face the daughter left behind — enter the daughter's brooding love interest from the wrong side of the tracks - her long lost brother? Or uncle..?

At eleven, Becky from accounting comes by with a huge stack of papers she calls 'the numbers'. I soon learn that punching numbers into a computer is more boring than having nothing to do, the way it keeps your mind in single file. I try to make the numbers mean something but they are the absence of thought.

Since Ari left, I've had a constant feeling as though something has been amputated from me, but worse — that what I lost was never there to begin with.

———

On Friday, the office takes the afternoon off to get started on some early drinking. Stepping out of the building, a net of sun falls through the concrete sky. Country music and bales of hay spill drunkenly onto the sidewalk from the cowboy bar. The women have their tits up and out, the men wear cowboy boots under their dress pants. I remember the cowboy hat Dad made me wear to the rodeo as a kid, its tight elastic band that left a red indent on my chin, a little red plastic whistle attached to it, which a lady yelled at me for using too close to her ear.

I take a shortcut through the alley to the art museum park with the white rainbow light up sculpture.

'Bianca!' I spot her.

In flip flops and a tube top, Bianca looks summery, a light brown tan coating her arms and neck from playing outdoor volleyball. I feel a wave of self-pity in my grey work skirt.

I pass her the pipe. 'God I don't know how much longer I can take this job.'

The sun sneaks through the buildings and stings my eyes.

'Want to go to iHeart next weekend? We could do those pills...' Bianca suggests.

'Dad confiscated them, remember?'

'Oh, right.'

'Psych! I bought more. Let's do some right now.'

I take out my small silver pill box.

'Chill,' Bianca says. 'Tonight. At the fair.'

On my way back to the office, I stop at a new age bookstore and buy a big red Astrology book on relationships. It matches your birthday with other people's birthdays, but I can't remember when Ari's is. It's either October 9th or October 29th. I sit down at my desk and read both combinations.

Oct 9th/Feb 16th > Starcrossed Lovers: deep-seated fantasies, lifetimes apart, at first disaster strikes, but persevere and unlock the love of a lifetime.

Oct 29th/Feb 16th > Running the Gamut: a match made in hell. Emotions run wild, dark secrets arise, proceed at your own risk.

'Lux,' Becky pops her head in. 'The numbers?'

The Denver County Fair gates are guarded by two women with snakeskin arms. We smoke up behind a tree out of view, the scent of deep fry masking the reefer. I close the pills in my hand. Tonight, Ari won't exist.

'I have a headache,' Bianca says.

'Want some Ketrolac?' I offer. 'It's from Donna's boob surgery. I took a few from the medicine cabinet. They say they're the Cadillac of painkillers. '

'Maybe not,' she says.

We get our wrist stamps and click the revolving gate, merging into the slow-moving, gelatinous crowd. When I was twelve, Dad would let me bring a friend to the midway, giving us the illusion of freedom by allowing us to wander off for half-hours at a time. I used to get so excited I was almost manic — the rides, the games, the treats, the lights. Now it all feels a little sad and false. Where is the sweet spot between these two extremes, between overwhelm and boredom?

Bianca stops to buy a bottle of water from a booth. 'Do you want one?'

'Sure.'

Escaping the lingering evening heat and inside the casino, we drop our molly at a high top table, watching the zombies crank their slot machines like assembly line workers, their eyes blank, anesthetized, waiting impatiently for their thrills.

'This place is disgusting,' says Bianca. 'These people are all a bunch of drunks.'

The bigger my pupils get, the more I see. And then, standing beside the payphones near the exit I see Ari, staring right back at me.

'Lux!' I hear Bianca call. 'Where are you going?'

Walking briskly away from where Ari is standing, I just keep going, past the slot machines, past the blackjack tables, past the indigenous man in the wheelchair with no teeth.

'Lux!'

I stop and turn. Walking towards me with Bianca is Ari's brother Jonas.

'Why didn't you stop?' Bianca asks.

'It's okay,' Jonas offers. 'I understand why you walked away.'

Jonas has been hurt by Ari, too. The shorter, scrawnier version of Ari, Jonas wears a white polo shirt with thin black stripes, and a white ball cap. I feel a sense of comfort in his presence. Ari without Ari.

'I feel nauseous,' I say, the M kicking in. I chug my water as the three of us walk around the air-conditioned exhibits in the basement of the building. Knives sharp enough to cut brick, zippered children's clothing, wooden stamps with your name on them. My name is never there.

'What do you think of Jonas?' I whisper to Bianca, as he watches a knife slice through a tree stumps.

'I thought you weren't into him,' Bianca says.

'I mean for you,' I say.

'Oh, he's hot enough for *me*? Is that it?'

'That's not what I meant.'

'I think I'll pass,' she says.

But Jonas likes Bianca. I can tell. Maybe he thought it was a double date, that first night we all went out.

'You girls have such big eyes,' Jonas tells us.

We laugh, keeping our secret. An old woman at a slot machine smiles at us, shiny collector's pins spattering her lapels like she's been under fire.

We find a spot in the grassy area outside the casino where there's about to be a small concert and sit enjoying the leafy nighttime air as a crowd slowly engulfs us. Up by the stage, I spot Ari. He has his arm around a girl and is putting too much weight on her shoulder. Greasy-haired Mila from Rockbar.

Someone like her. That's who I needed to be.

I drift into the pain I thought the M would protect me from.

Jonas stands. 'My brother looks drunk,' Jonas says. 'I'd better go check on him.'

Jonas ambles over to Ari, his hands in his pockets. If only I were attracted to Jonas.

I stare hard at Mila's face, trying to rearrange it to make it beautiful, Ari shuffling drunkenly beside her.

'See?' says Bianca. 'Look at him. He's a drunk. Just like all those other drunks in the casino. He looks like a dinosaur.'

'A dinosaur?'

'Well, he does. He's so tall and gangly. And he's always wearing that ugly green jacket.'

I smile.

Bianca and I buy cotton candy and take a ride on the egg-shaped blue and yellow buggies that cross the midway on cables. The fireworks are starting now, exploding packages of disappearing rainbows. Bianca is tripping out, rocking slightly like a child, as she sometimes does. Our legs dangle from the sky-buggy as the fireworks peak, raining down in one final grand stream of colors.

'My mom's boyfriend beat the shit out of her last night,' Bianca reveals. 'He broke her ribs,' she says. 'One punctured her lung.'

I feel my own chest tighten. 'Oh my god. That's horrible.'

Bianca is going to see her tomorrow in the hospital.

'Do you want me to come with you?'

'No. She's too embarrassed.'

'She's not the one who fucked up.'

'No, she isn't.'

The darkness I lust for, Bianca comes from it. This is why I'm always the first to step towards it, and she always tries to step away from it, then comes along in the end.

A fight breaks out behind us.

'Not in my own country, flip,' the man yells, his friend holding him back.

'Stop,' I get up. 'Stop it! Stop fighting!'

The Filipino guy pulls out a knife. I step back as he's pounced on by security.

The man approaches me, lifts up my hand and kisses the back of it. He has a paranoid sex appeal, his eyes still darting from the frenzy. 'You're beautiful,' he says.

I take back my hand.

'I hate this place,' Bianca whimpers, the MDMA grinding her jaw.

We get breakfast at the Denny's on Santa Fe, then get kicked out for lying down on the booth benches. In the Denny's bathroom is where I see the blood, iridescent red in the neon yellow lights. It's not normal blood. My body must be off. Maybe it's the drugs. It has to be the drugs.

On July 17th, the stadium is packed, the late afternoon air a lake of fire.

BANKS, Major Lazer, Diplo, but also 90s bands like Green Day, Weezer, and Hole.

Under the perfect blue summer sky, Courtney Love is pale white, her hair peroxide blonde, her lipstick red like cinnamon hearts. She kicks her muscular legs around the stage, her yellow baby doll dress flying up, her arms dangling back in the blowing fans.

'Nirvana?' she screams into the mic, reading a guy's t-shirt in the audience. 'That was seventeen years ago.'

We stand as close to the front as we can among grabbing hands and hot currents of cologne, the wind aimed only at Courtney.

'Resistance is futile, bitches,' she addresses the crowd, putting a leg up on an amp, flashing her white lace underwear.

There's a deadness is her eyes that fuels her.

CHAPTER NINE

"You make believe
That nothing is wrong until you're crying"
Limp Bizkit

On Monday morning I try to befriend the beady-eyed chipmunk in the office across from me. Her name is Kathleen. At 30, she's younger than the rest of the staff. She tells me she doesn't have anything for me to do, but I can hang in her office while she works. I take a seat across from her. A Seattle punk station plays on her computer, several chats blinking expectantly at the bottom of her screen. The female punk voice shrieks:

Not beautiful like you. Beautiful like me

'I love this song,' she says, blankly. 'You've probably never heard it. Not really your style, I'm guessing.' She bites down vertically on all four wafers of a Kit Kat. 'So, do you have a boyfriend?'

I half-expect her to answer the question herself since she seems to know so much about me. 'Yeah,' I lie.

'Oh yeah? What does he do?' she asks.

'He's a construction worker. His name is Ari.'

'How old is he?'

'24.'

'What's a 24 year old doing with you?' she asks. 'No offence, but you have the body of a twelve-year-old.'

She passes me a glance.

'Alright,' she reconsiders. 'Maybe a fourteen-year-old.'

Her desk phone rings.

'Come hang with me anytime,' she says as I get up to leave.

'Thanks,' I bite my tongue.

Back at my desk, Becky from accounting knocks on my door. 'Lux, I heard you were free.'

She takes me up the stairwell to the floor above. It's empty — no people, no furniture, cords sticking out of the walls. She leads me to a room filled to the ceiling with stacked boxes and a single swivel chair. 'We downsized last January. These are the leftover files.'

'What do you want me to do with them?' I flick at my lighter in my pocket.

'Alphabetize,' she says.

'Okay.'

'Call me if you have any questions.'

She leaves me with the whole empty floor to myself, standing in the mess of papers and folders. Am I free, or trapped on this floor of my own? I walk to the window. Below, the city is infused with summer. Quadrants of trees and lawns specked with tiny dots of people. Life happening within the grid, within the lines.

For the next summer month, I sort files into boxes and stare out the window. A jail sentence with endless time to figure out my crime.

―――――

Cantec Energy Corporation, Cantel Communications, Mr. Emerson Cartel... I sit on the floor with files sprawled out in front of me, arranging them into manila folders with white sticker-tabs. The work dries out my fingers and leaves tiny paper cuts on my hands. Time doesn't exist anymore. It is no longer the structure of things.

I pour myself a cup of coffee in the staff kitchen on the floor below, and weaken it with creamers and fake sugars, but it's just a back-up motor that can't energize me when the main engine won't start.

Kathleen enters the staff kitchen wearing her usual blue satin scarf, her cheeks deceivingly rosy and jolly. 'Oh. Hey teenager.'

'Hi Kathleen.'

'How was your weekend? How's your creepy boyfriend?'

I'm not sure if her monotone is put on, or if she's that square.

'Okay I guess.'

'I went to a show. I'd invite you sometime, but you know — it's not all ages.'

'I have fake ID,' I tell her. Not that I would go with her — rabid little chipmunk.

'Oh yeah, I'm sure your dad would love that. Does he know about your man?'

'I guess. I mean, not really.'

'Well has he taken you out for dinner? Somewhere nice?' She pours hazelnut creamer into her Sex Pistols coffee mug and throws the brown stir stick in the garbage. 'Didn't think so. Poor kid.'

She's right. I didn't play hard enough to get. I didn't want to lose him.

'Stay cool.' She closes the mini fridge and scuffles back to her hole.

Back up in my tower on the 24th floor, I take a staring break; the city looks like miniature and make-believe from. Cars merge in rehearsed, synchronized motions, invisible workers behind the scenes keeping things running. Like me. Do people live like this? For how long?

Bianca and I start going to the bar more often. We wear short black skirts and tall black boots, and sneak in flasks of tequila in our purses, then do shots together in the bathroom. We even bring salt shakers. We have a new game. When the bars close, we walk off our buzz in the downtown streets, screaming to strangers: 'Somebody love us!'

It feels good not to be quiet. To be loud and obnoxious like boys.

As the days go by, I start arriving late and taking extended lunches. I prematurely spend my paychecks at the downtown mall as a reward for not quitting. Tuesday, I buy pink runners and wear them out the store, and hate them by Wednesday, so I get a diamond ring, just a small one and call it a commitment of self-love. Thursday, I buy a white baby tee, and pair it with a baby blue spaghetti strap dress and black thigh highs. Friday, I buy the matching bracelets to the ring. They jingle when I walk through the empty hallways under the oppressive silence of waiting machines. My style is shifting. Less Gangster Bitch, more Pop Sugar.

Friday afternoon, I leave early. Taking off my heels and putting on my flip flops, I hope the sun is still shining. I take the stairwell a few floors down so no one notices me leave, then catch an elevator from Floor 21. When I've made it through the atrium in the lobby and out the revolving doors: I'm free.

At a tourist's pace, my sandals smacking up at my heels, I push play on my 80s Playlist:

Starlight, Star bright,
    First star I see tonight...

Luckystar. Rewind. Luckystar. Synthetic twinkling sounds that were once hi-tech in the eighties, that once encapsulated how fresh and exciting life could be. Each time the song ends, the world becomes vividly dead again.

My car is parked in a pay-per-day rooftop lot. Today, I feel like a drive. Drinking a cold Dr. Pepper, I drive aimlessly, then park my car under a railway bridge, and walk into the fading sun, the cool nighttime air charged with an electrical buzz. The South Platte river water is deep black, among the stockyards and chimneys. No one is around, the workers off for the weekend. An ongoing hum oscillates among the factories, occasionally interrupted by a loud clang. The man-made dreariness of the place is peaceful. There is no pressure here to be happy. I question whether I should be alone here at night.

At the bend of the river, I take a concrete staircase up an overpass and watch the gentle rolling thunder of cars underneath. Hands in the pockets of my fleece jacket, I play with a crumpled piece of paper that's been through the wash, tracing its soft edges, with my thumb. I take the paper out.

Rose Timakaia. That time in my life just a blur now. I feel the sensation of Ari's cold hands up my back. All I know is that I'm still bleeding. Barely, but every day. Can something die before it's even alive? I wish I knew.

I drop the card into traffic and let it spiral down into the muddy black river, water spilling up the banks from the week's heavy rain. It overflows. Bleeds like me for reasons it doesn't understand.

CHAPTER TEN

"God is empty just like me"
The Smashing Pumpkins

On Saturday morning, a final green Strath envelope comes — the bill. The cost of royally messing up your child per year? Twenty thousand dollars. So those five months I spent making minimum wage at Starbucks actually cost ten grand.

I fasten my rollerblades and skate to the park. Stopping at the playground, I throw my backpack at the chain link fence. It feels good. Temper tantrums are not a nice way for a girl to act, especially not a girl like me. I'm not homeless or starving or sick or even ugly. I have more than enough of what I need, I'm told.

I take large, awkward strides in my plastic encased feet over to the trash can and chuck my kilt into the empty metal bin. Before adding the blazer I take my pocket knife and cut out the crest, putting it inside my backpack. I light my Strath tie like a fuse. The uniform catches fire.

I skate all the way to the edge of the development until the sidewalks stop and find myself at the edge of the city staring into an open field where bulldozers sit dormant. Past the clearing in front of me, frail ravines lay in tiers in the far-off distance. I step off the pavement and wade through the wild grass, my clunky feet half-walking, half-rolling me forward like an android. Across the field is a ridge. A glacial breeze from the mountains rushes up against my back.

The ridge is further than I thought, but I'm already half way across the field, the wind helping to push me forward. I look back at the sidewalk. Behind me and to my diagonal left an animal stands in the distance, an unleashed dog that's gotten ahead of its owner, gold in color, maybe a retriever. Looking more closely at the dog, I realize it's too big to be dog. What is it? A wildcat of some kind. A chill runs up my back.

It lingers threateningly between me and where I've come from. Does it see me? It seems not to. Yet.

Should I run? I can't. I'm in skates. If I take them off and start to run in my socks, the cat would notice the quick movement, maybe even pounce. I calculate the danger of the situation. I've stranded myself here in the middle of this open field with weights on my feet. And while the field is so close, just next to the suburbs — it's not the suburbs. Though barely — this is the wilderness. I've never seen a wildcat. What is it? A cougar? Lynx? I keep my eyes on the cat to make sure I'm not hallucinating. I wish I was.

The cat stands in place, looking around and licking its paws. These cats are hunters. Tight with fear, I begin to cross-step slowly back, keeping a safe distance from the animal, an instinctual decision. I take slow steps, one eye on the cat. It could see me and attack at any moment. No one would hear me scream. My blood pulses.

When my skates roll onto the pavement, I delay my relief and keep skating against the wind.

Friday again. I try to spend my weekends wisely enough so I'm left with something to chew on for my following week of solitary confinement. As I leave work to meet Bianca, the weight of the building rises from my shoulders as I step into the street. I tell no one about the wildcat because it sounds like a lie. I begin to question whether it really happened myself. Strange how the things that happen when no one is around seem unreal.

I drive to Starbucks to get Bianca after her shift. Her parents have been crack addicts for most of her life. It's hush hush and sometimes the only indicators of them relapsing are the television going missing because her dad pawned it, or her mom ending up in ER.

'Turn left here,' Bianca says.

The apartment complex we pull up to is dirty white with bars on the basement windows. We take a dodgy elevator up to the second floor, the pickled scent of old tobacco permeating from the gaudy hall carpet. The guy, Bernie or Benny, Bianca can't remember, barely opens his door to hand us a white envelope, then closes it before we can pay. We look at each other, the TV blaring inside, and shove money under the door.

We park the beamer in a pay lot and sit cutting up the blow, watching people go in and out of the bars.

'Why have we never done this before?' I ask, cutting the coke into lines with my debit card on an ipad, the way I had watched Reese do on his parents' pool table.

'We need to get rich,' I say. 'Let's plan a heist.'

I pass her a twenty and she does the first line.

Across the street, girls huddle in line in their heeled boots, their coats covering the length of their miniskirts, making them look naked underneath.

'Do you think there's something fundamentally off about this world?' I ask, doing my line in one swift motion, the chalky swell hitting the back of my throat with a numbing cool.

'I don't know.' Bianca flips down the passenger mirror and puts on mascara.

I don't how people don't see it.

A limo with kids going to their prom after-party drives by. A girl hanging out the window with champagne in a peach satin dress, baby's breath in her hair screams: "so long, suckers!"

'Oh yeah, I got my dress!' Bianca tells me. 'It's purple with sequins.'

'Sounds... nice,' I say. To be nice.

Sounds like a bad situation.

'Do you wish you went to prom? Just to get dressed up?' she asks.

'For who?' I ask.

A fight breaks out on the street outside the bars, a nearby cop car sounding its siren to quell the uproar. I watch the pushing crowd entangle itself.

Bianca doesn't need to know things like I do. Maybe it's the ones like Bianca who make it, and the ones like me, who can't accept things the way they are, who don't.

Monday. My alarm clock penetrates my dreams in the form of breaking glass. My eyes sting, my stomach is a clenched fist, my head feels depleted, I've overdrawn my stash of dopamine. Once awake, I remember where I am, *who* I am, and feel like crying. I have to get up. Now. And make myself look nice, then race half the city downtown. How have I kept this up for so long? I jerk my head under the covers and pout like a child.

In the mirror, my face is missing its usual glow. This is the last straw. I can suffer physically; it's no sweat. But my face is not something I'm prepared to sacrifice. All this said, I'm fairly sure I'll talk myself into it again. Drugs are a mind game. Thought vs substance. What's the one magic thought to once and for all trump my dirty little habits?

8:30 AM. Pop radio plays from an office phone while I sort a stack of manila files that look almost soft enough to be a pillow. The same songs over and over. Beat 107 Plays Today's BEST Music!!!!! They brag, over and over. Songs so processed that even if they once meant something to someone their meaning is now lost, the lyrics bought and sold. I sing along to stay awake. Why would the universe send me a wild cat? An occurrence too large and strange to be passed off to chance. Maybe I was meant to face off with the cat? Maybe the cat symbolizes Ari. Danger. Stay away, stay out of sight. All I want to do is forget about my love life, but all I hear broadcasting across America are constant reminders that everyone else is in love and singing about it. I rip the cord out of the wall and throw the phone across the room. A large chunk of drywall falls over the broken phone as it lands, its receiver in two clear pieces. Oops.

My mind scrambles for solutions to fix the hole in the wall. I could tell Dad one of the file cabinets fell. Or, I could just lean a file cabinet up against the hole and pretend nothing happened. They'll discover it months later and figure it's damage from the move. I wonder how long it would take them to figure it out. It could be weeks, the only time I ever see him when I get my glasses of Tang from the kitchen downstairs.

I press my weight up against one of the file cabinets, holding it close like we're dancing, but it's too heavy to lift. I manage to push the smaller cabinet over a few feet, inch by inch, and cover most of the hole in the wall, then do my usual slip away down the back stairway, even though it's only 11:00 AM. I'm a wake of destruction.

I change into my red bikini at home and pour myself a glass of lemonade from the mini fridge downstairs. I lay out a towel and feel the sun beaming down like it's going to lift me into a spaceship. Take me now.

'Lux,' Dad looms above me in his gardening gloves where I suntan in the backyard, his spade pointed downwards at a dangerous angle. I've fallen asleep in the backyard. I press the backs of my hands against my cheeks to feel if I'm burnt.

'You're home,' I say.

Crap.

'I came home to change and these weeds caught my eye. Why aren't you at work?'

His glare is fixed solidly on me, as he takes his gardening gloves off.

He doesn't get it. I'm not at that point, of shaping my actions towards goals.

'I had a panic attack,' I come up with.

He scans my face, but my sunglasses shield me.

'Lux, we all have to work. You have to be responsible. You have to grow up.'

I hate the loser he thinks I am.

'Whatever,' I reply, not strong enough to fight back. I roll over onto my stomach. I'm done with this Rapunzel gig.

He stands over me, blocking my sun. 'What are you going to do now, Lux? Lie around and smoke grass all summer?'

'No one calls it that,' I tell him.

'You're going to ruin your beauty.'

I gather my things, triggered yet relieved.

'You have to do *something*,' he says.

I could tell him I'll get some other job. That everything will be fine. But I'm so weak right now. I wish he would just leave me alone.

'I'm just... sad,' I say. The most honest thing I've said to him in years.

'About what?' he asks, exasperated.

God forbid I be depressed. Depression, everyone knows, is contagious.

―――

At night, I dream about a bunny caught in traffic. I retrieve it and set it free in the wilderness where it belongs, but it runs back onto the highway and sits staring at me between the speeding cars.

With Dad away on business, I've been sleeping fourteen hours a day since I quit, though my sleep has been anything but restful, with dreams of knife fights and wildcats. In one dream, I'm making out with a statue of Ari, and I know he isn't real but I don't care. I shouldn't be here, at home. The real world is working away, doing things that need to be done. But I can't care.

Home has become the opposite of home. It's the place I least want to be. But with all the hours I put in at the firm this summer, I don't have a dime saved. No money to move out, or even to go out for an evening. It's all been funded towards easing the pain — clothes, make up, alcohol, drugs, partying. Hell, if I had the money, I'd pick up a gram of coke right now.

I take my dad's tennis racket down to the outdoor tennis courts down the hill and smash the ball against the back board again and again. But the ball is too bouncy, too hard to control. I stop myself short of throwing the racket and slump down against the back board, closing my eyes. I'm spiralling.

What do I do? Go to Bianca's? She can't help me this time. Call Ari? He doesn't want me. His image is sewn into the lining of my every thought, and I'm nothing to him. How could I even think of going back to him?

I could call Shawndy. Leopard-print slipper Shawndy. Was she serious when she said she'd help Bianca and I out if we were ever in a jam? Is she a headcase, or just eccentric? Does it matter?

'Shawndy. Hey, it's Lux.'

I sound down, she says, calling me sweetie. She invites me to meet her at Starbucks. Uneasily, I accept. I don't want to know anyone right now. And I don't want anyone to know me.

CHAPTER ELEVEN

"Diamonds deserved, diamonds but he convinced me I was worth less"
Lauryn Hill

A sickly moon sits like a flaw in the sky, craters revealed in its yellow light. I sit by the window at Starbucks waiting for Shawndy, shielding my face with the brim of my baseball cap.

Why didn't I just call Bianca? Bianca is useless to me right now. She's too vulnerable herself to help me. Behind the counter, Phoenix is bent over fiddling with the espresso machine. I pass her without saying hello. Shawndy shows up late, giving me a bear hug in a purple faux fur coat.

'I'm so glad you called, honey! Look at you! You're so pretty. Just look at those eyebrows,' she says in her smoker's voice. She orders a latte and buys me a frappuccino, but when she looks at me she can tell I'm not well.

'Let's get out of here,' she says. 'Meet me at my place.'

There's a word I'm looking for, as I enter Shawndy's house, past her graffitied shed, upon which someone has scrawled: '**I have AIDS**'.

Seedy. This is the word I'm looking for.

Shawndy makes no mention of the red spraypaint as we walk into the house. Stepping inside the back door, across from the coat rack is a calendar of naked women flipped to a Marilyn Monroe look-alike blowing a kiss. November.

'Well, this is my happy home!'

Strippers magnetize themselves to the side of the loudly humming fridge, their names italicized: *Candy, Sammi, Stacia.*

'Sorry about the mess,' she says, feigning shame for my presence.

She walks through to the living room, Hustler magazines haphazardly spread across the coffee table, throws off her coat, puts her hair up, and does a sun salutation. 'Make yourself at home.' She pats the white leather couch. 'Stay the night. Stay as long as you want.'

'I didn't bring face wash.'

'I'm a girl boss. Haven't you heard? I have samples.' She digs some packets out of her purse, then prepares a bong filled with ice and two glasses of iced tea.

With each bong hit, I float through the everlasting gobstopper of my bad mood

'So. Tell me everything. It's a man, isn't it?'

'I thought so,' I say. 'But maybe it's me.'

Shawndy withdraws a small bag of white powder from her coat pocket and lights a cigarette. 'I could see it in your face. Your body language. He's taken your spirit.'

The smell of her burning cigarette calms me as she carves the powder into lines over a pair of largely inflated breasts.

'They act up and you really feel for them, ruining all they've got.' She exhales a ribbon of smoke '...but that's not love.'

I braid a strand of my hair. 'It seems like the way life is supposed to feel – I can't feel that way on my own.'

'It's hard to connect with people who don't even connect with themselves. I've been seeing this guy, Brett. A jazz musician. Irritates the hell out of me with his sanctimonious self-promotion. Some people don't know they're born.'

Shawndy fiddles with the lines, evening them out. 'Those of us who do wake up, who want more — they beat us down. We're the dangerous ones.'

'Who is *they*?'

'The ones who rule this open prison. The illuminati.'

'What's that?' I ask, searching it up on my phone.

'You're cute,' she says, fluffing the leopard-print throw pillows. She takes a sip of her drink. 'Actually, I've got just the thing for you, sweetie.'

I expect her to pass me the rolled-up bill, but instead, she dives onto the floor and opens a cabinet full of porn DVDs and Disney movies. 'Here.' She hands me a dog-eared paperback book.

The Hatred
How Love Kills Slowly

I eye it over — feminist pop psych?

'Now,' she says. 'Do you want some of this?' She hands me the Hustler magazine, white lines censoring each nipple.

After Shawndy has gone to bed, I lie on her couch flipping through the stack of Hustlers. Reese used to keep a porn collection at the back of his closet behind his school ties. I found it once while hiding the remote. But as much as Reese thought he was a stud, he never made a move on me, apparently only able to handle sex on glossy paper. I pick up the Hustler with the circus theme — girls on elephants, with whips, and hoola hoops, and rings of fire. At the back of the magazine are 1-900 numbers advertised in small square boxes, 'Barely 18' the one that catches my eye.

This what I was to him.

My chest collapses. There is no love, nor was there ever.

I pick up the paperback book. It begins with a story about Jessica - a suicidal 20 something. Overweight, unkempt, and suffering from anxiety. She describes her boyfriend, Kayden, who she's deeply in love with: he buys her flowers, holds her hand, takes her on expensive vacations… Then one night at a dinner party in response to an interjection she's made, he tells her to *shut up*.

The exact same words Ari once said to me.

Humiliated, Jessica felt. To be shamed in front of people like that.

He's charming, but switches on a dime. He's caring, then swiftly cruel. He wears her down, day by day, making her think it's all in her mind.

Do I suffer from drug addiction?
Depression?
Crying spells?
Anxiety? the book asks.
From the outside looking in, it might appear that way.

"Women like assholes."

"Women are suckers for punishment." They say.

Hardly. More like they are desperate to escape the pain, but they've been raised to accept it since they were young. Little girls groomed for mental abuse.

Was I taught this?
I thought I was sheltered.

"Being with him made my world come alive. He was infatuated with me, and I adored him. Then suddenly, he would be disgusted with me for no reason. I didn't want to see it. He was so loving, then so hateful. Slowly the pain overtook me. I took off the blindfold and saw the truth: he hated me. Nothing could water down this hard truth. Nothing could explain it away."

~Jessica

Did I rationalize things? I tried to understand them.

What feeds her addiction? The high. The dopamine triggered when he shows her the ultimate attention. She craves her next hit, willing to give up more and more for it. Willing to give up anything.

On our trip, I gave up my expectation of him to behave like a normal human being.

I thought that once we got to know each other better, our relationship would naturally develop. That if I could just be myself around him, we could understand each other.

I skip to Chapter 6:

Is your love really hatred?

> *Jessica hated herself. She thought that if she made Kayden happy, their relationship would be smooth sailing. But Kayden had no interest in an equal partner. When he got too close to Jessica, he would lose his sense of power. So he denied her feelings, because they reminded him of his own. He took away her self-esteem. That way Jessica could never leave him.*

So Ari was afraid of me? Afraid of losing me? That doesn't seem right.

Everything becomes clouded again. If Ari was so set on controlling me, then where is he now? Control doesn't let go. I skim the book for an explanation. There is none.

At the top of the trailer park, a breeze circulates, cutting up one way then swirling back the other, messing up my hair. It's still a summer breeze, mild in temperature. The trailers have flimsy white siding, surrounded by vegetable gardens and plastic white lawn furniture. Permanent temporariness. I hold my hair off my face and stare at mountains beyond the city.

'Hey trailer trash,' Bianca says. 'I rolled this joint as your back to school present. Go ahead. Spark it.'

I wet the joint with the underside of my tongue and burn off the twist at the end. Bianca will be working at Starbucks full time in September and I have to finish my GED.

'Okay, here's the plan,' I tell her. 'Meet back here in ten years with whatever kids and furniture we have and get a trailer.'

'Kids? I thought we were kids.'

'Not anymore,' I break the news.

We sit for a moment on the ridge, letting the wind whip our hair around.

'Do you think Ari hated me?' I ask Bianca.

'Nah,' she says. 'He's just fucked up.'

Maybe it's that simple.

I feel that twinge of pity for him that I always mistake for love.

On the week before school starts, Cayce calls me three times.

Each time I see his name come up on my phone, I shake with rage at the thought of Ari giving him my number. One day I decide to pick up. I don't care if Cayce drops dead, but I want to know how is Ari doing without me. Cayce rambles on about his bike. He's shy and it's unattractive.

'So, what's Ari up to these days?' I ask.

'I don't know. I don't see him much lately,' Cayce says. 'He's always with his girlfriend.'

My heart snaps like elevator cables. 'Oh? Who's his girlfriend?'

'You met Mila, right?'

I freeze solid. I thought Mila was a shoulder to lean on. Not an actual option.

Cayce is still talking.

'Look, I have to go.' I hang up and block Cayce's number.

How long has he been with her? Was he with her while he was with me? I feel like I'm going to be sick.

All the time I spent thinking about him... Everything I did to figure him out. I throw myself onto the couch, knocking a pile of books off the coffee table. I'm so stupid.

Slowly, her rage turns towards herself.

Mila is a slob. She's gross. A bottom-feeder. Is this better or worse than the untouchable Trina? The idea of Ari being with Mila dissolves everything I thought I knew about him.

I lie on the carpet. I will never get up from here. I may eventually lift my body, but my mind will be in this same place for a very long time.

My hair is washed and curled for my first day back at school. It bounces as I walk down the community college halls — happier for me than I am for myself. I wear a white skirt, and a purple printed top with white pearl buttons and white wedged sandals. I will register for my courses here in this orange brick building from the 70s, and will come here for tests and materials, doing most of the course work online. It will feel good to put this behind me. I sometimes have pangs of regret for not getting it over with when I had the chance, but at first, dropping out, I felt more alive than I'd ever felt. I guess it couldn't last forever.

I watch other students meeting with their teacher's aids, leaned forward with determination. And then there's me, disoriented and faded.

My T.A.'s name is Matt.

'We'll be working with a lot of graphs and formulas...' he tells me '...trigonometric equations...' he's saying.

He has a gentle presence with a soft tone and soft blonde hair. Matt might have once known sadness.

I drive home, looking for Ari in passing F150s, and wonder if he can feel me hurting. I crawl back into bed, hoping the sadness won't find me, but it does. I dream of Mila. She's on the phone with Ari, her back turned to me. I try to scream to him that I'm there but he can't hear me on the other end. I wake up to the sensation of Ari's arms wrapped around me, his hands warm and sorry.

What ugliness inside him attracted him to her?

'You sleep too much.' Dad peeks into my room.

'Not now.' I say.

He gently closes the door, then opens it a crack. 'I'm going out for dinner with Donna,' he says. 'I'll bring you back something.'

I wait until I hear the finality of the garage door closing, then get up to put on Led Zeppelin and open the book. I keep it in my top desk drawer, each night reading small sections. It's the methadone to my heroin. I make myself some tea and try to do my math homework, but pounding disinterest throws itself in front of every equation before I can solve it. I curl up by the window and lose myself in a novel - Ignorance, by Milan Kundera. The book is about how you can never go back. It's supposed to be sad. I find it comforting.

On Monday, I tell Matt I won't be able to do the course because 'I'm going through stuff'.

He looks concerned with his big teacherly eyes.

'It's okay,' I comfort him.

'Can I be of any assistance?' he asks.

I shrug.

'You must be an artist,' he says, crossing his padded elbows, leaning against his desk.

'What kind of artist?'

'Exactly. What kind?'

I get the point. And I'm grateful for his rare humanity in this world. I consider having a crush on him, but a gold wedding band gleams up from his crossed arms.

I call Bianca from the parking lot. 'I'm quitting my GED.'

'Shocker,' she says. 'No offense.'

I envy her for having no expectations heaved upon her.

'You're not going back to him, are you?'

I consider the words: going *back*. I'm not going back, per say. We do have unfinished business.

'I miss him,' I admit.

'Lux - how can you miss someone you never really knew?'

'I don't know,' I say. 'But you can.'

CHAPTER TWELVE

"I went down to rescue you. I went all the way down"
Courtney Love

On a rainy November Sunday, I pick up weed from Della while Dad and Donna drink coffee and Bailey's and listen to Michael Bublé. It has been over two months since I quit my GED. I've been going for long walks, reading self-help books, and eating a lot of pasta. Bianca has been hanging with her public school friends, Bernadetta and Sharice, who are back skeazing on the bar scene after having their babies. Public school life.

I have to get a job. But to serve people, you have to sell yourself every day. I have nothing to sell. I can barely be bothered to enunciate my thoughts inside my own head, let alone speak to others. It's for this reason that Bianca and I have kind of stopped talking.

'It's too much effort...' I try to explain. She doesn't know me as I am now, having forgotten how to be 'on'.

She interprets my explanation as cruel — that she's not *worth* my effort.

I don't have the energy to soften the blow. So we leave it at this.

I apply at a dive bar called Cyrus where VLT addicts and alcoholics go to waste their lives. I want to work somewhere where I can look like crap. Lynette is the manager — a smoker with a sticky-looking perm and an ass the size of an old TV.

'No gym clothes', she points to my hoodie.

'No stretched out tattoos,' I mutter when she walks away.

Cyrus - perverted old men, Guns n Roses, flat beer. The best thing is the second-hand smoke, leading me to an early death. Wiping down ashtrays in the back at the end of my second shift I decide to never come back.

Falling into a light sleep in my Cyrus apron after a dinner of cold vegetarian pizza, I jolt awake and try to put a name to the sensation lurking in my body as I brush my teeth. I turn on the sink full blast and scrub my face with a washcloth, turning the tap off just as the water dangerously kisses the rim. If Ari was the catalyst for me becoming this sad person, the source of it all, then he might hold some clarity for me. I dry my face with the corner of a bathrobe and vigorously put on moisturizer. Our energy is still intertwined.

She's learned to see drama as an essential component of love.

The book shakes its finger at me from the back of its drawer. I retrieve the book — insight into Ari's bag of tricks:

Getting Sucked Back In
He's not that bad
We have so much fun together
It hurts me when he's hurt
I've put too much into this to just walk away
I can't live without him

I may have invested my virginity in him, but my real reason for seeking him out is none of the above. It's about taking control. Like a terrorist before a suicide bombing, I have nothing to lose.

Shibley. Ari is not on Facebook, but I see Jonas' profile picture, his small face always a comfort to me. I message him and he replies almost immediately.

Ari is living with their sister up in Elyria-Swansea, he says, always polite. He gives me Ari's new number and tells me to say hi to Bianca for him. A deep sense of peace overcomes me, knowing where he is.

―――

There was a nightmare I had when I was a kid of Stromboli, the puppet master from Pinocchio. When Dad would read me the book, I could never look at the page with Stromboli's fat, twisted smile. 'Stromboli came running…' he would read, and I'd close my eyes. In the nightmare, I'm walking along the street towards my house, but Stromboli is standing on the sidewalk blocking my way. I need to get past him to get home, so I walk right up to him, hoping he'll leave me alone, but he doesn't. He picks me up and begins repeatedly slamming me into the ground, whispering in my ear to never come back. When he finally lets me go, I stumble away, shaken and bloody, but I realize - I still need to get home. So I turn and walk back to my house where he's waiting for me just as he was before, and he attacks me once again. It was the most frightening dream I had ever had. I was terrified of him, and I knew I couldn't stay away.

I pace my room as the first snow falls arbitrarily outside. Dad's in Acapulco for a golf trip. I have to do it. Now. This is the time I've chosen. Six o'clock — dinner time, the time he'll most likely be done work. I dial. 720-876-253………4.

It's ringing. Too late to hang up now.

'Hello?'

'Hey. It's Lux.' I try to sound friendly.

He's stuck. He has to talk to me.

A woman's voice hollers his name in the background, offset by yapping dogs. His sister?

'I thought you fucked off,' he says.

'Look… do you want to meet up?'

'Where?' he asks.

Where. Not no.

We make plans to meet up at Roma Pizza.

He was always there, the whole time. All I had to do was call.

Hanging up the phone, I go to the mirror and smile. I'm okay now.

From this moment on, I'll be okay. This small action I've taken, however it plays out — *this* will change me.

I know I can do it now — whatever it is I think I shouldn't.

Sitting across from each other in the little red booth at Roma Pizza, Ari and I are exactly as we were in the beginning. We face each other with the same charged withdrawal, that same strange attraction between us. I've ordered apple juice. The first few sips singe my insides. Ari has ordered a beer, his head tipped back watching the game on a screen behind me.

'Hey.' I snap my fingers.

He looks at me intently, eyelids drooping with apathy. 'Did you know you're beautiful?' he asks.

'How's Mila?' I respond.

'Look... that was never at the same time as you. How's Cayce? Huh?'

'Ew? How would I know?' I feel that hurt again — how he handed me over like an outgrown toy. 'I can't believe you gave him my number.'

He leans over the table. 'It turns my stomach,' he says in a low voice. 'To think of you two together.' He runs his hand across the edge of the table as though he's built it himself. 'I kept looking over and seeing you talking to him that weekend,' he says. 'We never had that, you and I.'

Part of my hurt evaporates. Jealousy - something I understand.

'I was never interested in him,' I say. 'Not at all.'

He resumes watching the game, hot pizzas gliding by on massive trays.

'So you're living with your sister?' I ask.

'Angie kicked me out when I started drinking again.'

'What about Trina?' I ask.

'Trina stopped talking to me after that day.' He finishes his beer.

'What day?'

'The day we came to Starbucks. She said I was sick for dating you.'

I laugh.

'What can I say — even my girlfriend hates me. She just doesn't understand what it takes to make a relationship work.'

My stomach tightens against the swishing apple juice poison. *Girlfriend*. But moreso, it's his mention of the word *'relationship'* that floors me.

'What did you do to her?' I pretend to play it cool, feeling utterly stupid for reaching out.

'I left you with a pretty bad impression of me, didn't I?' Ari smiles, shifting to the corner of the booth. 'She's mad because I'm leaving to go to New York for modelling in the fall. So I guess that's it for us.'

Ari, a model? I guess he has a look. I always thought he was beautiful. Apparently he knew it, too.

'What about you?' he asks. 'Do you have a boyfriend?'

'No.'

'Why's that?'

'My last boyfriend really messed up my head.'

'Oh yeah, who was that?'

I look at him.

'Well, I wasn't really your boyfriend,' he smiles.

The words sock me in the aching gut.

'You're sexy when you're pissed off,' he says.

When the check comes, Ari pays for our drinks and walks me to my car, opening the door.

'Thanks,' I get in, thrown off by his chivalry.

He slams the door shut with my hand still resting against the frame. I loudly draw in a sharp breath.

'Shit,' says Ari. 'I'm so sorry. I'm sorry...' a look of genuine remorse on his face.

'It's okay,' I say, before I've inspected the damage.

My hand throbs as he continues to apologize. It feels so good that he's sorry.

He holds my hand in both of his.

'It was good to see you,' he says, kissing me on the cheek.

I start my car.

Ari is so much weaker than I thought. This is the reason he can only meet my eyes with an impaling stare. It's not him I was obsessed with after all, just a feeling. I don't feel that way anymore, do I?

I hold my bruised, swollen fingers.

―――

Boots, a black cashmere sweater, tight jeans, and a black velvet headband. I walk into the pub conscious of my poise for the first time in months. It's busy for a Tuesday night — guys in their Carharts, waitresses in plaid kneesocks that make their calves look fat. Ari is playing pool. He looks really good and it catches me off guard. I always forget the effect he has on me in person.

Over the holidays, we didn't speak. My Christmas presents - Aqua di Gio, MAC make up, Bose speakers — each one opened was a sock to the gut. Not what I really wanted. Worse, I didn't know what I wanted. When I wanted Ari, I had a tangible goal. Guess that's why when I got the text begging me to come see him, I caved.

I watch him play, his shoulders curved over his cue, his torso leaning over the red felt table so comfortably. He misses his shot and looks up. He has a black eye.

He smiles. 'Guys, this is Lux.'

Tonight, he's jovial Ari.

'Nice to meet you.' I smile for them, my gaze looming over his eye.

'My ex-girlfriend punched me in the face,' he explains.

Ex.

'How are you?' he asks. 'How have you been?'

'Okay,' I reply.

'You look nice,' he says. 'What's wrong?'

Tonight, he's caring Ari.

'I just have to finish this game, then we'll go, okay?'

'You want me to go somewhere with you?'

'It'll be fine,' he says. 'We'll take a cab. I'll pay for everything.'

'Where?' I ask.

'My place.'

Going back to his game he looks back at me occasionally, like a little boy checking to make sure his mother is watching.

He has two faces and like the flip of a coin, she's never sure which face she'll get.

Ari leans out the Uber window and loudly sings:

She's got a smile that it seems to me, reminds me of childhood memories...

I tug on his shirt to reel him back in.

...where everything was as fresh as the bright blue sky

He screams the lyrics out the window, the look in his eyes mildly manic.

'Who knows what I could have been,' he rolls up the Uber window and suddenly gets dark. 'I work fifty hours a week just to pay for this shit life.'

'What about modelling?' I ask.

'I'm not going,' he says. 'Gig fell through.'

Ari's sister lives in a stucco townhouse. She's fallen asleep in front of the television, a large woman in a blue sweatshirt with crocheted slippers. Ari leads me down a dark staircase that smells like potpourri and turns on the lights to a room with a huge flat screen and three tiers of black leather couches. He struggles with the remote.

'When Angie had the second baby, she lost it,' he says. 'She got postpartum and kicked my cousin out. So I had to go, too. So I moved in here with Jenna and Dwayne.'

Ari pulls me on top of him. 'Lux,' he says, almost hoarse. 'Will you kiss me?'

I hold his eye contact, threading my fingers through the holes in an afghan on the couch.

He looks at me. 'I have feelings for you,' he says. 'It surprised me when you called,' he says. 'I never thought I'd talk to you again.'

I don't know what to say.

He rolls onto his side away from me. 'Fine,' he says.

He carries a lot of pain. I can feel it. I bring my lips to his and kiss him.

No matter how far he falls, she'll go down to rescue him.

He closes his eyes beside me.

'What's your birthday again?' I whisper. But he's already asleep.

Something has shifted. The first sparks of euphoria. Will it stay? Or will I have to go back to that place I've been for so long.

In the morning, I shake Ari gently awake. 'I called a cab,' I tell him.

'Okay, bye,' he kisses me with his eyes still closed.

I quickly kiss him. 'Cash?'

He said he'd pay and I'm holding him to it.

'Oh, right.' He opens his eyes, gets up, and walks me to the door where he hands me a twenty.

I wonder, as I kiss him goodbye, what else will he forget he's said?

———

The following week, I'm determined to set some goals and clear my head. I buy a yellow poster board from Staples and draw a large mind map of various careers. University Professor? I just escaped from school. Lawyer? I just escaped from an office. I just don't see a way out.

I sit on the floor of my room and stretch, then go to the kitchen to get a pitcher to water my one and only plant — a red and yellow tropical one that looks plastic.

'Where did you get this?' Donna asks, holding up the book. She's just gotten in from shopping, bags burying the counter with her shopping addiction.

'Did you go through my things?' I ask.

'Of course not. You left it on the coffee table.'

She wears a cream blazer with shoulder pads and has her hair slicked back flat and tight like an 80s power bitch.

'*Hatred*?' she asks.

'What are you, the librarian?' I grab the book out of her hands.

I've heard her tell my dad he needs to have better boundaries with me. How I'm spoiled, in not so many words. Well, I was here first, and I'll always come first. Sorry bitch.

Bianca comes over after school. We order pizza and make Christmas cookies.

'Don't wreck it,' Bianca says.

In some places I've rolled the dough too thin, the snowflakes tearing as I try to lift them onto the pan. I drop a red pearl of dye into the butter icing and a pink swirl forms with the whir of the mixer.

'So Ari called you drunk from a bar and he had a black eye from his ex-girlfriend and you went *home* with him?'

'It wasn't like that. He was being open with me. Being honest for once.'

'How do you know?'

'It's not like I slept with him.'

She slips one of the trays of cookies into the oven.

'So have you talked to him?'

I shake my head.

'Well,' she says. 'Now you know.'

When Bianca leaves, I put the snowflake cookies with pink icing in a container, small bits of shiny ribbon showing through its translucent sides, and, in snowy traffic, drive all the way to Ari's and leave the cookies on his doorstep before he gets home from work.

By 9:00, I haven't heard from him, so I call.

'I'm on my way out. Can I call you later?' Ari says. 'It's kind of a bad time. Mila and I were just leaving.'

Mila. The name descends like darkness as we hang up.

Have they been together this entire time? What does he see in her? I thought he'd sobered up enough to see her hideousness.

Fool me twice.

Well, he can eat the damn cookies and think about me with each bite.

———

I've been smoking up during every waking minute, so everything is fine. Della gave me a small glass bottle of oil. With Dad at a law convention in Phoenix, I burn it with two blades on the gas stove. It smells like burnt sesame seeds. I call Bianca.

'Want to come over?'

'I can't,' she says. 'I have to work.'

'Why don't you call in?'

I need someone here with me right now.

'What about when I need you?' she asks. 'You're never there for me.'

'Like when?'

'You know, he's just going to fuck you over and drop you again.'

She cuts deep.

'Forget it.' I hang up.

I do a few hits of the blades, bringing the hot knives to my mouth and inhaling the thin smoke streams, and put Led Zeppelin on the surround sound speakers on all floors of the house.

Close the door turn off the light
  No they won't be home tonight

I find myself lying outside in the snow, looking up at the empty, frosty sky. I've drifted away somewhere, smoking the oil. The cold seeps into my clothes as solemn guitar blasts from the patio speakers. This must be how people go crazy. They check out for a while and decide not to come back.

I get into the shower to warm up, the droplets shooting down my back like finely chiseled diamonds, the steam swallowing me in a cloud.

Scraping the last of the oil out of the bottle, I gently cross the border from stoner back to couch potato. Shift my dependence from drugs to television. But I can't watch anything about love. I surf the channels like I'm dodging a sniper — dating shows, no. Soap operas, no. Sitcoms, mostly no. I stick to the HGTV. Some talk shows are okay, but if there's any mention of weddings or dating, I grab for the remote. It's during The People's Court that he calls.

'I want my Tupperware back,' I answer.

'I thought it was a gift.'

'The gift was what was inside.'

'Thanks,' he says. 'For the cookies.'

'Why are you calling?'

'Come over,' he says.

'For what?'

'Because,' he says. 'I enjoy spending time with you.'

'And Mila?' I ask.

'She left me,' he says. 'Long time ago. Will you just come over?' he asks. 'I want to see you, Lux.'

Here he is coming to get me. But I'm exhausted. Destroyed.

I put on sweat pants and a baseball cap and get my keys.

On the way to the TV room in an open hall closet, there is an easel. On the canvas, the first tracings of an image and at the base, a photo of an ugly girl. Mila. Did he draw this? Ari walks past it without noticing or caring that I've seen it. Every time I think I know him, he becomes someone else. This sensitive side, can I ever get a slice of it? Or is it only for greasy-haired swamp creatures with grubby jeans? Then again, it was just an outline. An *urge* to paint. A feat given up on. Maybe the real Ari isn't capable of anything past its initial idea.

Side by side, not touching, we sit on the middle black leather couch while Ari's sister and her husband watch the news upstairs. As the movie plays, I find myself dry heaving at the love scenes. I have conditioned myself out of love.

He pauses the movie and leans in to kiss me. I lean back away from him, causing his outreaching hand to knock my ballcap to the floor.

'What?' he asks.

I reach down to get my hat and replace it on my head.

'There is no such thing as romance with you.' Ari moves to the other end of the couch and lights a smoke.

'I want more than romance,' I tell him, curving the brim on my hat.

The movie on pause, Ari examines his cigarette. 'You don't want to be with me,' he says. 'I'm a disease. I ruin people's lives.'

I nod.

'I just don't know if you can handle me,' he says. 'I'm not good at loving people.'

Seeing that I'm upset, he pulls me onto the floor on top of him.

There *is* romance, I want to show him. If he only knew what went on inside me when he touches me. Perched on top of him, I wipe my eyes with the backs of my hands. He traces a line down the middle of my chest.

I let him look at me.

CHAPTER THIRTEEN

"It was so much easier before you became you"
Sheryl Crow

Ari is bad at loving people. He just got out of a relationship. He needs time, he says. But the more time he takes, the more I feel like being with me is his last choice. That all the girls he really loved are gone and now, there's just me left.

Meanwhile back at the ranch, Dad eventually realized there was no forcing me to finish my GED, then gave me a $1500.00 IKEA gift card, and kicked me out. I will receive a thousand dollars a month to pay the bills. I can see that his guilt is through the roof as he tells me, his eye contact anywhere but on me. It may all be Donna propaganda. I heard her say to him: 'you shouldn't have to walk on eggshells in your own home.'

'Everyone else in your class graduated,' he told me.

'This is true,' I agreed.

I have always internalized his tendency to place the weight of the world is on my shoulders and I have always felt like I should be able to hold it up. Now, I see it's a grand lie he's telling himself. He'll tell himself anything to avoid seeing me for who I really am.

I could promise to shape up. I've been meaning to. But like a monk, I'm intrigued by the idea of living on nothing. I want to know what it feels like.

So March 1st, I move into a second floor suite in an apartment building in Speer, an older neighborhood with reaching trees, messy gardens, and wandering cats, defying my linear suburban upbringing. The building has a white pebble finish streaked bronze from the rusted window boxes. When I arrive, nothing has been dusted. This place will never be home. What have I done?

I get a new job at Roy Rogers to subsidize Dad's monthly cheques. We talk once a week. I'm fine. He's also fine.

I walk to work, spring coming too late and too slow, snow clinging to the shadows. But for each day the sun shines a little brighter, I stay the same. I haven't heard from Ari in months, but I feel him inside me. I take the alleys so I can cry on my way to work, the crunch of the gravel muffling the sound. I use my gloves to stop my mascara from running, making sure to wrap it up before I get to the bridge.

Roy Rogers has arcade games, darts, and even a bowling alley. It's a very fun place, I've been told. Brick exterior, freakshakes, hipster nonchalance. We wear navy t shirts and large marigold ribbons in our hair, and on Wednesdays, we're supposed to wear sports jerseys so I'm now a San Jose Sharks fan. I learn the POS system, memorize the beer menu, and try to become a better actor.

"I like your bag," my co-worker Marnie says.

I transplanted my blazer crest onto my black velvet crossbody satchel, an amulet to mark my escape, like a hunter wears the tooth of a shark.

'Thanks,' I say. 'Thrifted.'

Everything is wrong. Things I never had to think about in Country Hills. The water in my shower arbitrarily switches between scaldingly hot, forcing me to jump back against the tiles, or piercingly cold, which I heard is good for you. The fridge door won't close properly. Even when I make sure it's stuck shut, I wake up in the morning to find that it's peeled open, my orange juice lukewarm. And every morning I wake up to the gargantuan pacing of my upstairs neighbor, his gait more apathetic than angry; I can hear the obligation in the way he moves. My romanticized notions of being poor have been disillusioned, and it only took a few weeks. This is not the kind of poor you play at when you're a kid, stealing cans of beans from the pantry and pretending to cook them on the furnace.

On Monday, I speed walk to work, dodging people's refreshed spring glances. On the bridge, a boy stares through one of the cement, caged window-holes. He drops down a penny and watches it fall into the water. Like a beauty queen, I wish for peace.

I get to work fifteen minutes late. The floor manager, Pamela, approaches me to reprimand me, but feels my forcefield of apathy and is brutally rebuffed, telling me only that my closing duty is to do roll ups. There are six of them; they sit in their office and watch us through strategically placed cameras. If we ever stand in one place for too long, they call the phone in the bar and suggest things we could do like empty all the ketchup bottles, clean the bottles, then put the ketchup back in.

The lunch rush is weak today. I make less than $50.00 in tips. There are so many other things I could be doing right now. Not that I would be doing anything but getting high, but still. It's the idea of people deciding for me how to spend my time.

After the rush, my co-worker Marnie and I sit in a back booth doing roll ups. She tells me she's saving up for a boob job. She's short and tanned, and has bright, shiny pinkish-red layered hair. I guess she's flat, but it's not something you see when you look at her.

'People get braces if they have crooked teeth. So why not?' she says.

We roll up the knives and forks tightly into the green cloth napkins.

'I've always worked,' she says. 'I'm the kind of person who likes being busy.'

Life is easy for her. I can tell.

'No offense, but you look miserable here,' she says, stacking the rolled napkins in the bin. She shrugs. 'There are work horses and there are show ponies.'

I have to stop smoking weed. It's making me ugly. I take my stash out of its small Mother of Pearl container and flush it down the toilet, then immediately regret it. Weed has been my strongest weapon for so long.

I put on uplifting trance and unpack the rest of the boxes from my closet. Then stop. I don't think I will fully move in after all. I'll just camp here, until the time is right. My lease is month to month; I could leave at any time. I have a sensation that something is about to happen. I follow this feeling.

The next morning, I go to the bank and apply for a credit card as a birthday present to myself.

The teller is not much older than me. She has her life together, with laminated brows and winged liner. She asks me about my income, my age, my current address.

'Well I'm not sure how long I'll be there, but...'

'That's not something you really want to say when you apply for credit,' the teller says, more out of incredulity than as a word of advice.

'2787 Logan Street,' I tell her.

I didn't realize I was being judged. In the adult world, you must always assume this.

I walk out with five grand in credit — a pretty good chunk of change and even though it's not technically mine, it feels like it is. I'm high with potential power.

Dad's on a golf trip, but he left me a present at the house. My first Gucci bag. It's monogrammed and has a gold padlock.

Love from Dad and Donna, the card says.

I immediately want to destroy the bag, then consider that I could just sell it on Kijiji. Adulting.

Bianca texts me a screen of birthday confetti.

I reply t-h-x.

After working Happy Hour at Roy Rogers - tech start up guys in bad beards and selfie queens in mom jeans, Marnie and I go to a karaoke bubble tea bar called Very Merry Tea Day. Marine buys me a purple taro one with tapioca pearls. A few Asian men smoke cigarettes dipped in cocaine and sing sappy Chinese ballads off-key. I take the mic.

'Billie Eilish!' says Marnie. 'Or Ariana Grande Seven Rings!'
'I'm a 90s girl,' I tell the crowd.

It is a night for passion, but the morning means goodbye
  Beware of what is flashing in her eye

Marnie tries Bohemian Rhapsody and channels a fat Cajun woman, belting unabashedly. The Asian men clap, thoroughly impressed.

Spring pushes through the night air as we stand outside waiting for our Uber. There are so many places I haven't been. So many people I haven't met. But people never seem to be where I am. There is something missing between me and people. I don't want to famous or star in movies. I want my life to *be* a movie. A clear focused set. A sense that this is it. This is what's happening right now and nothing else.

On the weekend, I cave and call Bianca. Call it maturity.

She's sorry, she says, especially about that last thing she said.

'I know what I'm doing,' I tell her. 'Even if it doesn't make sense to you.'

'More than anyone else I know,' she agrees.

But I know now the attack she's capable of. Out friendship will never be the same.

I plan to meet her and her new boyfriend, Raj, at The Church where Raj's hockey team has rented a private room upstairs. Bianca and I take an Uber downtown in the mid-March sleet. She wears a strapless black onesie with ridiculously large hoops and a high ponytail, I'm wearing a mauve heathered dress and white runners and my hair in a bun and a white mini backpack.

'Did you lose weight?' she asks.

'Food is expensive,' I say. I've been getting by on veggie patties and banana smoothies. My fridge doesn't keep food cold anyway.

'I have to say I'm surprised. I thought you would have run back to Daddy by now.'

'You underestimate me.' I cheers her with my can of green tea Hey

Y'all. It's impossible for me to keep people at an arm's length. I'm not one to hold back, even if she's changed in my eyes.

Once inside the club, we cut through the drunk college kids to a winding staircase behind the stage. The small hidden red room is abuzz with twenty burly hockey boys jumping on plush red furniture. They've been drunk all day. The chandeliers shake with the rumble of the room. On the back wall is a fully stocked bar, but no bartender. Bianca introduces me to Raj, a smooth skinned South Asian guy with big muscles. He puts his arm around her.

'Would you ladies like a drink?' Raj goes to get us drinks from the bar.

'Pretty hot,' I tell Bianca. 'But his shirt is a little Jersey Shore.'

'He's okay,' she says. 'For now.'

Raj returns with two Hey Y'Alls. I can't tell if he's flexing his pecs, or if they're always like that.

'Thanks, babe,' Bianca says, still shy around him.

I hear a bottle smash in the bar and look back to see a guy standing on the bar ledge pouring booze into two girls' mouths. He empties the bottle over his chest, then rips his shirt open with his hands.

Raj shrugs it off. He's seen it all before. Wild parties with hired girls, no doubt. He has the look of a cheater.

'How's work?' I ask Bianca, Raj's heavy arm draped over her bare shoulder.

'Not bad. How have you been?'

'I need a vision quest,' I say. 'Maybe I'll drop some more M...'

'Magic career pills?' Raj laughs.

The red room pulses like a heartbeat. In one swift motion, the guy with the ripped open shirt wipes the bar clear of all its bottles. A scene from a Tarantino film on some cutting room floor. The glass shatters with muted sounds on the red carpet. Through the red tinted window, I look down at the far away glimmer of the drunk college girls' jewel tattoos on the dancefloor. They're alive in a way I notice only because I'm not.

Just because I can't smoke it anymore, doesn't mean I can't still get high off it. Actually, I could get a cleaner high if I eliminated the smoking part. I remember Shawndy saying that you just have to ingest a larger quantity than you would smoke, so I pick up two grams from Della and bake it into two very large chocolate cookies. As they bake in the oven I worry about whether I've added enough. Lifting the tray of cookies out of the oven, the weed smells like broccoli.

Still warm, I take a bite of one, hoping the chocolate will overpower the taste of the weed. Nope. Tastes like fertilized grass. I choke down the cookie, suppressing a few gags, then sit and wait for the weed to kick in, nibbling at the second in anxious impatience, just in case. Queasiness swishes ruggedly inside my stomach and a strange dizziness sets in until I can't see.

I would have been smart to throw up. But the last thing I remember before crawling into bed is a pallor bordering on a shade of green staring back at me in my bathroom mirror.

My thoughts disconnect from one another. In a hallucinogenic fever I had when I was eleven, the ceiling of my room stretched stories above and the homes across the street began to lift and churn like a tornado. This is the closest I've ever come to that sensation. I fall into a coma-like sleep that continues through the night and late into the next day, at which point, I wake up for a few seconds and fall back asleep.

When I wake up, I can't lift my head off the pillow. I turn my head to look at the clock. 5:00. AM? PM? The sun sits half-dark in the sky. I've overdosed. I immediately feel stupid. Overdosing on *weed*? Who does that? Why didn't I get it out of my system?

I couldn't have. I had no thoughts.

I lie pinned down under the covers by invisible rocks. Above me, my neighbor lumbers in frantic steps. Back and forth, back and forth. The walls shake. Is he building a temple, transporting bricks across the room in a wheelbarrow? Bands of censored winter sunshine plow in through my blue velvet curtains.

I fucked up. Shame surrounds me.

I limp to the bathroom, folded over like I'm 90, and hold my mouth under the tap. I splash some water on my face looking in the mirror. I've developed his stare.

Having already missed a shift, I see the missed calls from Pamela and assume I'm fired. I stay in bed for three days.

I've done permanent damage this time. There's a discordance in my brain.

'Smile,' the businessmen tell me as I take their order.

As I turns out, Roy Rogers is short-staffed and I must have sounded so awful on the phone that they believed me that I'd been sick.

I offer the table a mouth smile and gather their menus.

Loading my tray with their six mugs of beer, a leftover wave of dizziness from my overdose hits. The tray becomes light in my hands. I feel it tipping. Cold beer douses my forearms and the carpet. The businessmen clap.

Wanda, one of the assistant managers, comes out of the back having caught the accident on camera. She gestures to the mess, looking at my hairline instead of my eyes. 'We need to clean this up,' she points out.

Thanks, tips.

I turn and walk back to the kitchen.

'Lux!' she calls after me.

I run down the back stairwell, my purse and coat flying behind me, my apron full of cash abandoned on the expo line.

On the bridge, I dial Ari's number.

He picks up.

'Can you just tell me...'

Her okayness is based on his presence in her life...

'Tell you what?' he asks.

...his is based on control.

'Never mind,' I say and hang up.

Walking home, I stare down at the black river under the dark March sky, rushing towards nowhere. A rain turning to hail starts to fall. I enjoy the way it stings my face.

The number comes up like a winning lotto pick.

'I just feel like I'm special to you...' he says.

'You are special,' I say, so purely that it becomes true.

'I don't get why you love me,' he says. 'But I'll try.'

I take a deep breath and savor it like candy.

I sit across from him so polished and clean I can smell my own perfume — a musk and orange peel scent. At the risk of being short on rent, I've spent the day at the spa getting a facial, manicure, and pedicure. For my outfit, I've chosen a cinched, paisley halter-top and a pair of tight white pants with red velvet flip flops and a ruby locket of my mom's.

'You've got a great ass,' he says.

Not really the compliment of my dreams, but a nice change from 'legs'.

He orders three beers, the calamari, and an 8 ounce steak platter. I tell him I'm not hungry and order stuffed mushrooms and an amaretto sour.

'Come with me when I go to New York in the fall,' Ari says.

'You're going?'

'I have a new agent,' he says. 'She has connections.'

'I can't,' I say.

'Why?'

'I have to go back to school,' I make up a reason.

Once I've said it, it makes sense. I have to finish my GED. I have to go to college, even if I have no idea what I'm doing. I don't see a way around it.

'Fine,' he says. 'Don't come.'

The tab comes to a hundred dollars.

'I guess I'll have to treat you next time, huh?' he says.

I feel like the squirrel in the bedtime story Dad used to read me who kept trading pieces of his shiny, bushy tail for acorns until he had no tail left.

After dinner we go back to my place. Ari walks around opening cupboards. 'Daddy's lowballing you, huh?'

Will he see me differently, now that I'm on my own?

'Shoddy workmanship,' he checks the baseboards.

We sit on the couch, holding hands and watch hockey

Later, falling down into my bed, I take in his scent as he wraps his arms around me. Laundry detergent — the scent of love. He starts to kiss me, interrupting me from savoring his essence.

'When you go to college, you're going to meet some guy and realize what a loser I am,' he says.

'I won't.' I lie on his baby smooth chest. 'Trust me.'

Slowly, he undresses me.

I stop him. 'But what about…'

'—If you get pregnant, I'll marry you,' he says.

He overpowers me. Floods my senses like a casino.

CHAPTER FOURTEEN

*"When they get what they want
and they never want it again"*
Courtney Love

I snap pictures of him in his sleep. Hearing the clicks, he opens his eyes a slit, then pulls my pillow over his head.

'I hate having my picture taken,' says the model.

Click - his brow clenched like a pouting kid.

Click – his glare cracked into a smile.

Two pictures. Proof of his existence.

He throws the blankets aside and gets up.

'Can I borrow your toothbrush?' he calls from the bathroom.

'…I guess so.'

I hear the shower switch on and make the bed, then go to the kitchen. He emerges from the shower clean with wet whiskers.

'I made you lunch,' I tell him. 'It's in the fridge.'

'What is it?' he asks.

'A sub sandwich.'

'No thanks. I'll grab something at work.' He puts his boots on. 'Can I borrow 20 dollars?'

Wow.

I can hear my neighbor crying through the ceiling.

'I guess so.'

Once he's gone, I hop in the shower, throw his lunch bag in my purse, and make my way to my new job. The Auto Auction is located at the southern tip of the city, the sun baked fields washing up right against its cement lot. In the morning, I drive the cars through the wash bay, the greasy wash bay boys shirtless under their jumpers, then in the afternoon I drive them through the auction, waiting in the parade of cars, then slowly pulling into the crowd of fast-talking auctioneers and tire-kickers in cowboy hats and ties. All I have to do is get in the car, close the door, and start the ignition, and I'm in my own air-conditioned bubble. The buyers meticulously inspect the cars, look under the hoods and in the trunks until an auctioneer smack the car's roof to say it's sold. But no one ever inspects me. I'm invisible in the chaos of yelling and bidding. I just glide right through. In the eye of the storm, the perfect place to hide.

―――

In the soft May evening light, I drive to the North East to meet Ari at a pub called Schepps. The pub is dingy with red plastic candleholders and studded leather chairs. Ari sits with another hot guy by the pool table, a beer on his knee. He comes over to kiss me on the cheek. 'Lux, this is Sam.'

Sam tips his ballcap to me.

'Sam's been working up on the rigs,' Ari says. 'I haven't seen the kid in months.'

Sam is good-looking like Ari but in a more boyish way — rosy cheeks, a blonde shock of curls, and a naughty smirk. Sam laughs as Ari makes fun of a man at the next table eating his fries with chopsticks. The claustrophobia I feel when Ari is surrounded by allies, by people who love him more unconditionally than I do.

'I actually can't stay.' I interrupt their bromance. 'I told Bianca I'd meet her downtown.'

'I'll come with you,' says Ari.

He's choosing me over his homie who he hasn't seen in months?

'Sam's playing baseball tonight,' Ari explains.

Ah. Of course.

On the patio at 56Thirty, young people sit under heat lamps and a sheer white awning drinking expensive drinks. Bianca and Raj sit across from Ari and I. Ari has taken an interest in Raj.

'How about a game of sticks next weekend?' Ari asks him, turning his head mid-sentence to check out our waitress.

I catch a look from Bianca - she doesn't want Ari near her boyfriend.

'Another round,' Ari orders from the waitress. 'And four shots of tequila.'

She has a deep tan, round high cleavage, and her make up looks like it was drawn on with a dry erase marker. I get up to find the bathroom to freshen up.

When I come back, Ari's hand is around her waist. I walk right past the table, Bianca offering a mild 'told you so' look.

'Lux!' Ari follows me out to the parking lot. He knocks on my diver's side window. 'Wait.'

'Why do you always do this to me?' I ask through the closed window.

'I was only joking around,' he says, drunk.

I start the ignition.

'Lux.' He taps on the window. 'I'm sorry. I don't know why I get like this around you.' His voice through the glass sounds like how my thoughts have begun to sound in my head.

I unlock the door, not willing to leave him here to further embarrass us both.

He gets in, smiling. He's won again.

'You're cute when you're jealous,' he says. 'Come to my company golf tournament with me tomorrow.'

'I hate golf.'

Dad made me take golf year round, even etiquette classes in the winters, hitting balls into nets and replacing fake divots in astro-turf.

'Come on,' Ari says. 'You'll be the prettiest girl there. My boss will want to dance with you.'

'I'm not dancing with some creepy old man.'

'You'll dance with him if he asks you to,' Ari says, drowsy from the booze, his weakness magnified when he's drunk.

'I don't like you when you're drunk,' I tell him.

He stares through the windshield and goes to light up a smoke.

'Put it out,' I tell him.

He shakes his head.

'Put it out, Ari! Not in my car.'

He keeps it lit and smokes it down to the stub.

The next morning, I get dressed in golf attire while Ari lies sleeping in my bed. Why do I always give in? I put on a pair of black dress pants, a black collared sleeveless shirt, and a black visor.

'You look hot,' Ari says, waking up. He kisses my neck. 'I like the visor,' he distracts me, pulling me towards him.

'I'm all clean and nice.'

'We're taking your car,' he says. 'My truck's bad on gas.'

'Then you're paying for the gas,' I say.

'Then you're driving.'

'Do you think I'd let you drive my car?'

The Saturday traffic is easy. The sun shines into the sky like shimmering tiles at the bottom of a pool.

'Can you go a little faster?' he asks. 'Women. I swear.'

'May I remind you that I drive for a living?'

'Pull up a bit,' he says.

'Why?'

'I want to check out the girl in that car.'

A solid blow. He knows right where to hit.

He grabs my hand and holds it. I pull it away.

'You're a bitch, you know that?' he says. 'You're a little bitch.'

Tears leak out the sides of my glasses.

With blurry vision I pull up to a gas station. Would he have treated Trina this way? He did, I realize. It's unbelievable that Trina - such a smart girl — took this crap from him for so long. Two years. How did she do it? I think back to her bulimia confession.

'I'm not going with you,' I tell Ari when he finishes pumping the gas.

'You're coming,' he says.

'No, I'm not. Get Sam to go with you.'

'No!' He slams the passenger door.

I dab my eye make-up in the rearview mirror, pulling my shades back down as I see him walking towards the driver's side.

'I'm sorry,' he says outside my window. 'I'm sorry, baby. I really want you to come.'

He's apologizing. For the second time in two days.

'Please,' he says. 'I'll be so good to you today. You'll see.'

'If you pull this shit once more, I'm leaving.'

He forces me to hold his hand.

'I would never cheat on you, you know,' Ari says. 'I'm not like that.'

It's within the rules, he's saying, the way he torments me.

The farmland north of Denver is yellow and blue and only these colors. Having stopped by his sister's place to get dressed, Ari drives my car in a Tommy Hilfiger shirt slightly too large for him, the loose collar revealing the spoon shaped indent where his neck meets his collarbone. An innocent place on him. As he drives a little too aggressively, and I pout, we are a cliché. An after school special.

'Hey?' he nudges me. 'I hope you're not going to be in one of your moods today.'

As we pull up to the clubhouse, the perfect boyfriend show begins.

'This is my girlfriend, Lux,' Ari introduces me to his boss, Mr.Navarro. He then introduces me to each one of his co-workers using the word *girlfriend*, and kisses me, holding his lips to my stiffly held cheek.

Little Bitch. The words echo.

An announcement is made that all the couples will be playing on different teams and that we'll be playing Best Ball. As we walk towards the course, Ari slides up behind me. 'You have no idea how bad I want you right now.'

I feel a jolt of electricity from his touch, followed by the sensation of being crushed.

Once she lets him demean her, he knows he can do it again.

'Are you okay?' Mr. Navarro asks.

'Yeah, I'm fine,' I smile with an emphasized twinkle.

'Good. Because we're on the same team,' he says.

I take a seat beside him in the little white golf cart.

'You've got one hell of a drive,' Mr. Navarro yells over to me when I take my first swing, my prep school talents shining through.

'Nice swing, Nancy,' Mr. Navarro tells the guys after their lousy shots. When the drink cart comes by, he buys us all iced tea. I'm having fun until I see Ari's team on the seventh hole.

'Are you really a couple?' Mr. Navarro asks.

'Of course,' I say, puzzled by the question. 'Why do you ask?'

'You've got a class and style about you.'

And Ari doesn't, he means.

Class - could this have been hammered into me by Strathaven? Style - I do have style.

'Thank you,' I say.

Style is an art. Maybe I should dabble, explore the art of style.

As we sit down for dinner at the clubhouse, Ari is faultless. If his company sees he can hold down a girlfriend, they'll trust he can hold down his job. Barbecue blurs the air as the sun sinks behind the perfectly groomed green hills. Ari buys me beer after beer to sedate me enough not to blow his cover. We sit and laugh with the other couples and pretend we're one of them.

Beside me, Ari lurches his head to stare at the waitress as she passes, a redhead with a full tray of drinks. The table tries to laugh it off, but we're all uncomfortable.

'You're gonna get it, Ari,' Mr. Navarro says.

But he won't. I'll let it slide, not wanting to embarrass him in front of his friends. Wanting us to have a nice evening.

By not confronting him, she shows her devotion.

I shake it off and try to laugh along with them, and as I'm laughing, I realize I've developed his laugh, his unfazed sneer. I stop laughing.

On the drive back to Denver, the yellow and blue countryside turns orange and purple with the setting sun. In a haze from the beer, I let Ari drive.

Back in his sister's basement, we lie in his bed, tired from the sunny day. Him in jeans and no shirt, me in just a T-shirt. In his bed — the place I've wanted to be for so long. He presses himself against me as I repress the day's tears.

'Lux…'

'No.'

'Baby…'

'Please just stop.'

'Okay,' he says. 'I'm sorry.'

And he leaves me alone. The nicest thing he's done all day.

'Ari!' Jenna wails as she flips on the bedroom light. 'You were supposed to pick me up from work two hours ago.'

It's dark. We've been sleeping.

'Get your drunk ass out of bed,' she yells. 'And tell your slut girlfriend to put some clothes on.'

She's hysterical in her Minnie Mouse sweatshirt.

Ari rolls over. 'Get out of my face,' he says.

'This is my house!' his sister screams. 'You signed a contract. I do your laundry, I wake you up for work… Come on, Ari - I don't even charge you rent!'

He sits up.

'Jenna, chill. I've got debt to pay. I forgot you needed a ride.'

'That's it,' she says, the folds of her face swelling up, her eyes dilated and furious. 'You're out of here, Ari. Get your stuff and go.'

I look over at him, my heart pounding, and start looking for my clothes. I can't find my socks but put my shoes on anyway.

Ari grabs a piece of paper from his dresser, throws his clothes in a duffel bag, and stomps up the stairs. I follow him. How ironic to be called a slut when I've never been more frigid.

'This is what I think of your contract,' he tells Jenna, tearing the paper up and throwing it in her face.

'Get the fuck out!' Jenna yells. 'I'm done with you.'

He storms out, slamming the door, forgetting I'm still inside the house.

On the way to my place, I squeeze Ari's knee as he drives, knowing what it's like to get kicked out, to feel displaced. 'You can sleep at my place for a couple days,' I offer.

Silence.

We lie in bed watching TV, and he starts kissing my neck. The tears return.

She becomes so distraught that she has no love left to give.

'I hope you realize that when you're like this it causes more problems between us,' he says, shutting off the light.

He feels betrayed when she doesn't give him everything.

CHAPTER FIFTEEN

"Nothing left to say
And all I've left to do is run away from you"
The Smashing Pumpkins

Waiting in the car for Ari to finish his photoshoot at the modelling agency, I think of ways to leave him. It's hard to picture; this thing has been going on so long. *50 Ways to Leave Your Lover...* Doesn't matter how I guess.

An hour and a half goes by as I play on my phone. I consider being angry with him for telling me he would only be 'about 45 minutes'. He's ruining even this for me — hanging out in cars.

As I sit here, waiting to drive him around like I'm his chauffeur, I realize I'm not only this - I'm his shoulder to cry on, his bank when he needs a loan, his punching bag. I'm being used. Ari has made the mistake of giving me too long to think.

Finally he comes out of the studio, make-up smudged on the sides of his collar. He's never looked so hideous.

'What took you so long?' I ask.

'Shut up,' he says offhandedly, flipping through his headshots on the hood of my car.

The words resonate at a low, wavering pitch like the pressure before an ear infection.

'Move over,' Ari says. 'I'm driving.' He walks over to my driver's side door.

I get up, stunned by the blow, and let him drive.

'We're going out with my friends, tonight,' he says. 'Gabby, Josh... you know them.'

I do. And have been dreading running into them again.

'I don't feel like it,' I tell him.

'You're spoiled,' he says. 'You always expect to get your way.'

The interchange of forbidden hatred: he acts out her anger, she acts out his powerlessness.

Ari steps hard on the gas.

'Easy with my car.'

'Watch it,' he warns me, holding up a hand.

'Ha!' I laugh. 'What's that supposed to mean?'

He takes a corner too fast and clips the curb.

'Look, Ari, I don't need to sit around and watch you and Gabby hump each other all night.'

'You're jealous,' he smiles, delighted.

'Actually, you'd make a great couple. Her face is jacked up.'

He slams the brakes on and stops in the middle of Raleigh Street.

'Ari! What are you doing?' I yell.

With the car in park, he leans over, grabs my arm, and twists it behind my back. 'I could break your arm,' he calmly says.

The blow ups are only sporadic until she can no longer get free.

'I'm sure you could.' I shake my arm free.

He starts the car again.

'Look what you did.' I show him the red marks on my arm

'Don't be such a baby.'

She's not allowed to express pain.

I feel like I've been kidnapped as we pull up to Josh's house.

I don't want to get out of the car but I can too clearly imagine them all laughing when Ari tells them I'm out here pouting, again. I'm not that girl anymore. So I get out, to show them things are different between Ari and I now, even if they aren't.

Unlatching the back gate, Ari and I find the group sitting in Josh's backyard on folding lawn furniture, the same stuff they brought camping. It's like a reoccurring nightmare. Josh, Channel, Malcolm, Reuben – they're all here under red and orange backyard lanterns, beckoning me back into hell. No Cayce, at least.

Gabby comes running out of the house. 'Damn baby, you look fine!' She wraps her arms around Ari's neck and he lifts her up in a twirl.

'I hope you don't mind,' Ari tells Josh.

Take two.

I smile through re-introductions as I plan my escape.

Once again, I have nothing to say to these people. The silent girlfriend. The mail order bride. I can hear their thoughts:

'Can you believe she's still with him?'

'Poor girl.'

I tune back in to one of Ari's sermons, his crowd hanging off his every word 'That blonde newscaster with the hairsprayed bangs? Sure, she's doable,' he says, hubris spewing.

The friends laugh. They love the shock and awe of his antics, and he loves the accolades. I try to deafen myself without sticking my fingers in my ears.

Reuben invites the group to go skydiving next weekend.

Gabby laughs haughtily. 'Count me out.'

Ari is all in. 'Hey, I'd be fine ending it all right here. One last wild ride.'

He'd rather kill himself than be with me, is what he's telling them.

'You don't mean that, Ari.' Reuben tosses him a beer.

Chanel sends me a glance of pity.

All this time I've been trying to pump life into Ari from my own beating heart as though I had enough blood for both of us. Kids bounce on a trampoline in the neighbor's yard, their squeals of glee unmarred by the real world.

'Psych.' Ari laughs. 'I couldn't. I love my body.'

I can't even look at him. I focus on the line where the stubble of his beard meets the smoothness of his neck. It used to be my favourite place on him.

His friends laugh canned laughter. He scares them, too.

There is no feeling of accomplishment from seeing these people again. Ari is not my goal achieved. He's not my soul mate. He's not even the person who's hurting me.

———

Lying awake in bed, I can't help but wait for the feeling of his cold hands against my warm skin. This is exactly what I have to stop wanting. After Josh's, I dropped Ari and his yes men off at a club, telling them I had a headache.

'Okay,' said Ari. 'Leave the door open.'

He's living here now, I keep forgetting. Since the blow out with his sister.

In bed, I try to distract my body from craving him by replaying the night's events, but it's not enough. 'There are plenty of fish in the sea,' I remember Trina's advice. I drift off and wake up several times in the night, my heart clenched too tight to beat. It's five when Ari finally crawls in beside me, the sun just about to crack. He reeks of whisky and smoke.

'Don't touch me,' I warn him.

'What do you mean? I just want to lie here beside you.'

He's in that place again, the one where he's another, softer person. I can hear it in his voice.

'You're my girl,' he says, holding onto me.

Never once has he professed his feelings for me with confidence. Only in weakness, when he feels desperate for someone to love. It's the fear in him I've been loving as he says these things. The sight of him without his power.

He brushes the hair away from my face. 'What's wrong?' he asks. 'Tell me. You can always tell me.'

I face him, not wanting to let the opportunity slip away.

'You don't treat me right.'

He's silent.

'I know,' he says. 'I've been working really hard lately.'

'It's not that,' I say. 'It's the way you are.'

'What do you mean?' he asks. 'You mean my drinking? I know. I have to cut down.'

'No, Ari. It's the way you are to me.'

I let the idea soak in like the whisky in his system.

'Just like my father,' he mumbles, rolling onto his back apart from me.

'What do you mean?' I ask.

'I'm just like him. We're the same.'

The next morning, as he's shaving, he pulls me against him so I'm standing in front of him, both of us facing the mirror. He puts his arms around me and looks at our reflection.

'Can you make some coffee?' he asks, still half-asleep.

'I don't drink coffee, remember?' I tell him as I get dressed. 'I don't have a coffee maker.'

'It's not that hard to make,' he says.

So when I walk down to the corner store to buy bagels, I pick up a tin and look up How to Make Coffee without a Coffee Maker. While the coffee is brewing, Ari comes into the kitchen, fresh and clean and ready to go.

'You left the fridge open,' he says.

I put away the cream cheese and close it, then hand him his bagel and coffee.

He takes a sip. 'This is disgusting,' he says, getting up and dumping it down the sink. 'How hard is it to make coffee?'

'Why don't you just leave then?'

I dump the entire pot down the sink.

'You want me to leave?' He looks at me with doubt, waiting for me to take it back. 'Fine,' he says when I don't.

He goes to my room to get his things and puts on his shoes at the door. I do a round of the apartment, retrieving anything that's his: a pair of sunglasses, a black jacket. Now he has no reason to come back.

'Here.' I hand him his stuff.

'So that's it?' He realizes what I'm doing. 'Just like that?'

'Yep.' I stand in the doorway with folded arms.

'You're just going to stand there and watch me leave?'

I stand perfectly still.

Angrily, he tosses his things in the bed of his truck, screeching his tires as he speeds off.

I sit down on the steps and start to cry.

Inside, the phone rings. I follow it inside. 'What?' I say, in tears.

Silence. This is his apology.

I take it, unsure if I want to end it like this. Here. Now. And he knows he has me.

'Do you want to break up?' he threatens. 'Because people break up everyday.'

'No,' I tell him, the receiver hot against my ear. "I just don't want this."

'Then no more mood swings, okay?'

He denies his part of it, rewrites history to make himself come out blameless.

'Or you'll be short one boyfriend,' he says.

Seeing that he can press the reset button shows him he can attack again.

'Want to come over?' I ask Bianca, burgundy polish drying on my toes. 'We could make rootbeer floats.'

Since I OD'd on the cookies, I haven't been smoking weed.

'I can't,' she says. 'Raj is taking me shopping.'

Bianca has shifted her dependency from me onto Raj. For the best; it was weighing me down.

'So what, are you in love with him now?'

'I don't know,' she says. 'He's nice. He bought me flowers the other day,' she says. 'Roses.'

'Original.'

She tells me the Starbucks gossip - Jeffrey's wife has been stealing from the tip jar. Dallas is assistant manager now.

'How's your mom?'

She sighs. 'Back on the rock.'

'Oh,' I say in sympathy.

'Brit broke her arm jumping off a deck,' she changes the subject. 'She's giddy because her crush signed it. Oh, and I ran into Shawndy the other day at the store. She was sitting at the counter with some guy and then she just ran out crying.'

Shawndy, with all her ratchet wisdom, still going through it.

I tell Bianca about Ari and I, about our big fight.

'Lux… remember when you left that night at 56Thirty?'

'Yeah.'

'Well, Ari said some things when you were gone.'

'What?' I ask, unable to pin her tone.

'Well, I know he was pretty drunk, but...'

'What?'

'He said you're so sweet...' she hesitates.

'Okay.'

'...and… he said that he doesn't know why he can't love you.'

I sit down on my bed.

'I asked him why he keeps messing with you then. He said he'd never leave you.'

Is she saying all this to get me to dump him? Whether she's saying it to get me to leave him, or whether he meant it — doesn't matter. I don't need incentive. That was never the problem.

I tell Bianca I'll call her later. Hanging up, I lay my heavy head on my pillow.

Why does he want to be with me if he doesn't love me?

———

Driving home from the Auto Auction, I stop at McDonald's and pick up three orders of McNuggets for Ari. He'd probably love a coffee, I figure, so I make a quick stop at Starbucks.

July has hit and the summer air is thick and lurid. Ari has moved in with Sam in Aurora in a duplex, sleeping on a single mattress on the floor. Has he ruined my summer with his ruinous nature? No. Summer will always be mine.

My old Starbucks weighs me down with familiarity as I pull into the parking lot. Where it all began. I look for traces of the feeling I had at the beginning when I would delight in the uncertainty of not knowing when Ari might stop by. I stand in the short line and find myself looking around for him, the earlier version of him. The one I knew not as much about.

As though materialized by my own nostalgia, I look over to see Trina sitting at the counter. I haven't seen her in over a year, since that day when Ari pitted us against each other. There's something almost giddy in me at the sight of her. I want to tell her everything. Only *she* would understand. Inching forward in line, I watch her read the paper and drink her coffee. Her black hair has grown out into two tones, the roots a lighter copper brown. She wears a black t-shirt with a white skull on it and a leather spike bracelet. I will her to look up, but she doesn't see me. I know she hates me. All I'm unsure of is the degree of hatred.

Once I've purchased Ari's coffee — tall, black, one pack of raw sugar - Trina still hasn't looked up, her nose buried in the paper, learning, bettering herself as usual. 'Trina,' I say her name.

She looks up, unsmiling. She had already noticed me.

I wonder if she remembers that I don't drink coffee, seeing the large steaming cup in my hand. If she knows who it's for.

'Hey,' she forces, then leans back down into her paper. I'm owed no more than this.

Even though we were never friends, I guess she feels betrayed. I take the coffee and go.

Was he the same way to her? I feel connected to her at the mere possibility that he may have been.

In my car, I place the coffee in the cup holder and drive to Sam's.

How did Trina cut Ari from her life?

Well, I assure myself, however she did it, I'll do it better.

———

Placing the steaming McDonald's bag on the coffee table in front of Ari, I let him kiss me hello.

'Hi Sam,' I say, making sure to look at Ari as I say it, a trick I've learned to avoid a later fight. On the edge of the coffee table, a matchbook lies open in the ashtray. *Trina,* it has scrawled on it, *720-274-6681.* I pick it up, realizing I've seen it lying there before, the name only registering now due to her fresh presence in my mind.

'What's this?' I ask Ari.

'I ran into Trina at Schepp's a while ago. Why didn't you get sweet and sour sauce?' Ari asks.

A low-lying admiration I've had for Trina the entire time erodes. Trina hasn't freed herself from Ari after all.

'Sauce?' Ari asks again.

'Sorry,' I say absently, my mind already wondering something else — if Mila has also not really disappeared from his life.

'So what did Trina have to say?'

He laughs. 'Trina doesn't want me, but she doesn't want anyone else to have me either. Once you've driven a Ferrari, you'd sooner walk.' A sly grin comfortably spreads across his face.

He eats his meal, watching TV.

'I'm out,' Sam gets up.

'Where to?' asks Ari.

Sam winks.

Ari turns to me, 'Sam scored twins last night. What a baller.'

I cringe. Not about Sam's twins, which I doubt, or even that Ari is congratulating him for it. It's Ari's behavior in my presence — he doesn't care what I think of him.

I watch Sam walk out the door. They're friends for a reason.

'What movie did you pick?' I ask Ari, my eyes grazing the matchbook.

'You probably won't like it,' he says.

'So why did you get it then?'

He shrugs and starts the movie on Netflix, some action movie, then flops down onto the long part of the L-shaped couch. I lie down beside him.

'Do you have to sit so close?' he asks. 'It's a big couch.'

I move to the other side of the L and get a blanket.

'What are you doing?' he asks.

'I'm cold.' I wrap it around myself so he can't touch me.

He pulls it away.

'I can't have a blanket?'
'No.'
'Why?'
'Because you're annoying. That's why.'

Stab. His words hurt with the same strength and fiercer than the first time he ever put me down.

'You're lucky I can even stand to be in the same room as you,' I say.

He gets up and turns off the lights. 'Shh…' he says. 'It's starting.'

Hot quiet tears slide down my cheeks in the dark. I turn my head so he won't see them. If he finds me annoying, then I know at this very moment that he must, in some way, hate me. Not just *not* love — *hate*. Then again, there's no way he can hate me. He doesn't even know who I am.

———

On the single mattress shoved into a corner of his room, Ari pulls my white v neck sweater over my head. I blankly allow him to undress me like a doll. I'm used to it — give him what he wants.

The affection quickly fades unless it's entirely on his terms.

He tosses my sweater aside among the crumpled clothes that lay strewn over his bedroom floor, my bracelets clinking together as he slides them off my wrist. They land mutely on the carpet.

'Well,' he asks, lying on his back. 'Aren't you going to hold me?'
'No.'
'Okay,' he says after. 'You can go home then.'

I bring my arm across his chest under the tight stretch of the sheets.

'Too close,' he says, pushing my arm away. In the dark, his elbow hits me in the face.

I bring my hand to my head where he's struck me, tears sliding into my ears. *Why am I still here?* I shout the thought inside my head.

'You're still too close,' he says.

Suddenly, the orange streetlight shining through the blinds is too bright. I get up, upset, and try to find my clothes among his in the orange and black shadows.

'Leave,' he says. 'I'm finished with you.'

I flick on the light to hurry the process and say nothing as I get dressed, closing his door behind me.

I walk past his truck in the driveway, but have no urge to slash his tires this time. I'm not mad anymore.

———

To make it real there needs to be some words. I walk down the hot sidewalk. I've been walking aimlessly for hours, the heat sizzling up at me, unbearable unless I keep moving. I'm wearing sunscreen, but it's futile against the sun. Every few blocks, guys not used to seeing bare legs after the endless winter whistle and catcall. I don't look up.

Every step I take feels like a step in the wrong direction. Each passing car vibrates my core. Ari has been blowing up my phone. I would have killed for that a year ago. I can't seem to call him back. I keep dialling him and hanging up before it rings. I dial again.

'Where have you been?' Ari answers his phone. 'You just don't call me for three days?'

'Ari...'

'What's his name?' he asks.

'What are you talking about?'

'What's the guy's name?' he asks. 'Huh?'

'Who?'

'Your new boyfriend.'

He slams down the phone.

It rings a second later.

'Well, you know what?' he continues. 'This is horse shit and it's not going to fly with me.'

I hear, through his reprimanding, a slice of panic in his words. He's afraid of losing me, trying to scare me into staying. What he doesn't know is that I finally see: I never had him in the first place.

'Ari...' I say, dimly. 'I don't make you happy.'

'You can't make me *happy*,' he says. 'There's no such thing.'

'There's more than that, Ari, and you know it.'

'Why are you being like this?' he asks, his tone still hostile but now genuinely confused. 'You don't even sound like yourself. You're throwing these tantrums all the time—'

'—what do you call driving away screeching your tires, huh?'

'Are you finished?' he interrupts me. 'Look, if you wanna be together, we're not having these fights anymore. Anyway, you left your bracelets here.'

He doesn't get it. I'm not coming back.

'I don't need them,' I say, and going against all I've been taught about winning despite all odds, I hang up.

I cry shallow tears. There are none left to shed, really. I've already been in mourning for so long. I imagine him taking my bracelets and crushing their cheap, pliable metal in one hand.

I leaf through my two pictures of him from that morning, one after the next — one angry, the other pretending not to be. There's one more thing I need to check to make sure he's really gone. I go to CVS and buy a pregnancy test. Because that would just be too ironic, to finally rid myself of him, then have his baby growing inside me. I take the stick out of its white box and read the instructions. 99% accurate. What good does that do? I wait out the twenty minutes.

Negative.

Did I use it right? I guess we'll see.

Being alone doesn't feel any different from being with him. Really, I've been alone this whole time.

The Auto Auction has offered me a job in the office, the white trash freak show just strange enough for me to fit in. As I get dressed for work one morning, in the hanging black of my closet, I see prisms of reds, blues, and greens, shining through — the color creeping back into my life. What a little thug I used to be — all black, all the time.

While packing up the last of my boxes into the white moving van, I find the yellow poster board with my soul-sucking career choices mapped out. I tape it to the wall to see if any of the options resound with me now: university professor, lawyer, event planner, journalist, entrepreneur, psychologist. Nope. Nothing jumps out at me. There may be some signs of life coming from event planner and entrepreneur. Maybe I could take a career counselling workshop. Note to self.

I vacuum and wipe down all the surfaces in the apartment until they shine. Always leave a space nicer than when you found it — a hippie camp counsellor once told me.

'Supper time,' I call my dad from the kitchen when he gets home from work. My old room is a mess, but I'm redecorating it anyway. It will have a royal blue blow-up couch and a gothic mirror and embroidered pearl pillows and a beaded curtain. I have a vision.

'Thai. My favorite,' he says, opening the white take out containers. 'But is it hot?'

'Extra,' I say, spice my new favorite drug.

We eat on the patio in the late August sun, a crisp breeze threatening to take it all away.

It's just better when Donna isn't here. Then again, it could be worse. If my dad were single and depressed, I might come home one day to find him high on blades lying in the snow blasting Zeppelin.

'How does it feel to be home?' he asks.

'Kind of weird,' I say, dishing out a spoonful of coconut rice.

At the kitchen table, the descending sun shines in my eyes as we eat. I get up to close the blinds. Dad pulls out his phone and etransfers me five grand to cover living expenses while I work on my GED so I can save my Auto Auction salary for a travel budget. Maybe Europe. Maybe with Bianca. Or maybe I'll meet someone. But I have a feeling I won't.

'Now,' he presents his serious face. 'What are *you* going to do for me?'

This is where I'm supposed to present a budget and a timeline for my unadulterated, raging success. But beyond my GED and a grab bag of community college courses, I really don't know the way.

'Let me get back to you on that,' I tell him.

'Touché,' he says.

I've inherited his slippery way with words.

I look Ari up on Facebook after dinner. He has a page now. His profile picture is a photo of him playing baseball, his white baseball jersey against his grey-blue eyes, a pure canvas for his dead stare. A wave of pleasure squeezes down through my chest like a swallowed apple. That familiar aroused hurt — a high and a crash at once. With minor sleuthing, I see where he's living now, only blocks from where I left him on his mattress on the floor.

Would it be a mistake to drive by his house? Or bump into him somewhere? Let him catch a glimpse of me so he can see how well I'm doing? How good I look? Maybe he's in love with me now, since those are the ones he loves, the ones who leave him. Come to think of it, he probably would fall in love with the person I am now. Finally. Too late.

In golf, it's called a gimme. Chance assumed in one's favor.

I step out onto the deck in my socks, overlooking the dying ravine, leaves turning amber and falling off for the year as the nights get colder. I love to watch it die, almost more than I like to watch it blossom. Purple streaks of evening sun shine onto the neighbors' homes across the valley of trees, each with their hidden family dramas. What would happen if tiny ramps and bridges were built between each house? If it was societally acceptable to set foot into each other's homes and observe each other's private lives, would we want to watch? I would.

ABOUT THE AUTHOR

Isla Kay is a graduate of The Banff Centre of the Arts' Wired Writing Studio and Toronto's Humber School for Writers. She has published short fiction with Twenty3 Magazine, SpotLit Magazine, SubtleTea, Two Hawks Quarterly, and 365 Tomorrows. She was a frequent contributor to The Calgary Herald's Books section, Beatroute Magazine, CanadaWide Media, and is currently the Editor of Kay Press® {The Dowry, Tryst with Destiny}. Listen to Isla's tracks *Secret Life*, *Jet Set*, and *Night Stars* on Spotify, Apple Music, & iTunes.

Made in the USA
Middletown, DE
15 August 2021